Keystone Kids

Also by John R. Tunis

IRON DUKE
THE DUKE DECIDES
CHAMPION'S CHOICE
THE KID FROM TOMKINSVILLE
WORLD SERIES
ROOKIE OF THE YEAR
ALL-AMERICAN
YEA! WILDCATS!
A CITY FOR LINCOLN

Keystone Kids

John R. Tunis

With an Introduction by Bruce Brooks

An Odyssey Classic • Harcourt, Inc.

ORLANDO AUSTIN NEW YORK SAN DIEGO TORONTO LONDON

www.HarcourtBooks.com

First Odyssey Classics edition 1990
First published 1943

The Library of Congress has cataloged an earlier edition as follows:
Tunis, John Roberts, 1889–1975.
Keystone kids/John R. Tunis; with an introduction by Bruce Brooks.
p. cm.
"An Odyssey Classic."
Summary: When two young brothers join the Brooklyn Dodgers, one
becomes team manager and is faced with the task of uniting a team rife
with dissension and prejudice against the new Jewish rookie catcher.
[1. Baseball—Fiction. 2. Brothers—Fiction.
3. Antisemitism—Fiction. 4. Discrimination—Fiction.] I. Title.
PZ7.T8236Ke   1990
[Fic]—dc20   89-38711
ISBN-13: 978-0-15-205634-6   ISBN-10: 0-15-205634-3

Printed in the United States of America

H G F E D C B A

Introduction

Beware: *Keystone Kids* is a trap. It's a trap of the best kind—smart, amusing, and painless—but like all traps it grabs you when you least expect it and doesn't let go right away.

It's a trap carefully designed for sports lovers, because sports lovers—writers, readers, commentators on radio and television, fans in general—have always been suckers for the clichés of personality and drama. It's so easy for us to take an athlete with an odd personality and round him off to the nearest even "model," instead of coming up with a genuine character sketch every time a new face pops up.

The best writers, of course, are on the lookout to avoid clichés. The easiest way is to invent characters so obviously unlike the models that no one is ever tempted to force them into roles. In *Keystone Kids*, however, John

R. Tunis gets around clichés in the most *difficult* way: he invents superb, fully-developed characters who are *very close indeed* to our preconceived models.

Thus we have the spunky ballhawk (Bob Russell), the coolheaded "manager on the field" (his brother Spike—together they're the "Keystone Kids"), the prankster pitcher (Razzle Nugent), the noble outfielder who exists on a higher plane than the rest of us (Roy Tucker), and so on. The familiar roles lull us; we're tempted to fall back on the thoughts and feelings we've had a hundred times before, enjoying the light little drama of the Russell boys' rise from being naive bush leaguers to tough stars. Sure, we say, we know these types of guys, and we know this type of tale. We get comfortable with our expectations.

Then Tunis springs the trap.

What a simple trap it is, too: Hey guys, says the author, here's our new rookie catcher. Name of Klein, Jewish boy, hits for power, good arm. Can really help the club. Okay, fellahs—play ball.

But the ballplaying changes around the presence of Jocko Klein. Sure, he hits for power, chucks a good ball—but he's *Jewish*. That changes *everything*, right?

It certainly changes the seemingly well-established characters of our old pals the Dodgers, right before our eyes. Without melodrama or force, but rather with a dark naturalness that gives us shivers, Bob's spunky energy becomes aggressive prejudice, Karl Case's jovial sarcasm becomes malicious enmity, Roy's silent, lofty leadership becomes a guilty aloofness. In a matter of pages our beloved Brooks—so predictable a few chapters ago—have become a band of strangers dominated by hatred and meanness. They lose their cool, and a lot of games into the bargain; we lose our self-assurance about their behavior.

All of Tunis's books are about the lives of people who happen to be athletes, not about athletics. More than any other Dodger novel, *Keystone Kids* puts the personal issues in the foreground, in cruel focus. Baseball becomes just the means for the Dodgers to torture Jocko, every game a test that shows up his failures and drives him to fulfill the taunt that "Jews are yellow." The players helplessly watch themselves create strife that destroys their ability to play this delicately balanced team sport; they lament their losses, but they cannot stop ripping Jocko and, thus, the fabric of their team.

The only cool head belongs to Spike Russell, the rather grim young player-manager who must eke justice and a winning record out his shambles of a club. But Tunis had trapped Spike, too: He cannot deal with prejudice the way we do today, smashing it with harsh righteousness, because to humiliate or mock his men would rob them of the rugged energy he needs from them on the diamond.

Here in the 1980's we grow impatient with Spike's seeming softness. We want him to crack some heads. And when he puts the responsibility for snapping the strife on Jocko—the victim himself—we *really* rebel: Let him lick his wounds, Spike, we say—*you* take care of the agitators. If the boys commit the crime of intolerance, *force* justice on them whether they understand it or not.

But Spike's intricate patience works, and Tunis's trap finally opens, and out pops a strengthened Dodger team and a surprised bunch of readers. True, we might wish for a little more chagrin on the part of the offenders, a little more cosmic punishment; they are too heartily rewarded for a simple about-face inspired not by soul-searching but by a couple of big hits from Jocko. We want to hear them recite humbling lessons about equality, brotherly love, and character. What we get is teamwork on the baseball field.

Tunis knows that great baseball teamwork is, after all, great teamwork. Trusting a man to execute a hit-and-run behind you means more than unnaturally worded expressions of brotherhood. The Dodgers express the reversal of their prejudice exactly as they expressed their initial hostility, through the thing they know best and do most avidly: playing baseball together. No symbolism. No quotable sentiments for guilt. Just a key pitchout, a double-play off a tough bunt, a clutch sac fly. Take your cuts, Jocko baby, way to be, save my ups.

Tunis once again resists the temptation to make his baseball world a paradise of metaphor. He keeps his story within itself, lets his characters work things out their way, and leaves open the possibility of quiet soul-searching during the off-season. The off-season is *their* business; in *Keystone Kids* the heat of real human beings in a pennant race is *ours*. As always, Tunis's restraint is the key to his universal quality: He knows that a great baseball novel is, after all, a great novel.

—Bruce Brooks

Keystone Kids

1

From the dugout where Grouchy sat, the whole field spread itself out before him, the diamond not a diamond at all but what it really was, a square with players at every corner. Save for the pitching mound which rose above his forehead, everything was on a level with his eyes. He swept a glance around the familiar scene, seeing things no one else could see because managing this team was his business, his life. Then, bringing the scorecard up horizontally to his nose, he waved it slowly to the right. Immediately and imperceptibly, the three men in the outfield shuffled over nearer the right field line.

The manager's gaze took in everything: Lefty, the pitcher, towering above him in the box, his glove hanging from his wrist as he roughed up the new ball; the Mugger standing truculently at the plate, swinging his bat; the poised runner on first; and last of all the two boys near second base. Especially those two who had made the team what it was.

In deep short the tall thin figure pawed the ground restlessly with his spikes and almost at once smoothed out the furrows at his feet. Then he leaned over, picked up a pebble and tossed it behind him, spit into his glove and banged it with his fist. From the bench Grouchy watched him. He was tense, alert, as he concentrated upon the man at the plate and the signals from the catcher. On second base itself stood his brother and from him came that strident chatter, the tonic which had kept them all on their toes, which silenced rival dugouts in the verbal exchanges of the bench jockeys, which had spark-plugged them all through the season and helped them into the lead. Because with the end in sight the Vols were in first place, two games ahead of the Crackers.

The pitcher leaned forward and rocked slightly on the rubber. Grouchy gripped his scorecard.

This next pitch could mean the game. The pennant, too.

Lefty took the signal and nodded. Instantly Grouchy noticed what no one else did. The boy in deep short raised his glove as if he were stroking one side of his face, and the youngster on second, without ceasing the flow of words for an instant, edged over quickly toward first. One person, old Schultz the coach, at Grouchy's side, noticed it also.

"That kid thinks his brother knows more than Joe McCarthy."

Grouchy agreed. "Sometimes he makes me think so, too. But I ain't telling him!"

Then the Mugger swung. There were two hundred pounds behind his swing as he caught the ball, sending it along the grass between first and second, well over toward the right. The Mugger started with the ball and so did the boy in the field. Only from his position almost two-thirds of the way to first had he any chance, and only a chance measured in fractions of a second, the chance that comes off once in a hundred times, the chance every good ballplayer takes.

He raced over, low, glove outstretched, and stabbed at the ball. He had it. Hardly pausing in his motion, he tossed it underhand, the only way he could, to the man on first. The first baseman jumped clear of the on-charging Mugger and burned the ball to second. The tall boy, waiting coolly, took the throw and put it on the base runner as he thundered desperately in. It was a doubleplay, *the* doubleplay, the most difficult, the most intricately timed play of all. The side was out.

They stormed jubilantly in toward the bench, the fans roaring. The younger boy, waiting a moment for his brother, exchanged insults with the Mugger, now returning slowly toward his dugout. Then his brother trotted up and the boy put one arm over his shoulder, turned to yell at the Mugger and, grinning over the applause, reached up and tipped the other's cap. The fans yelled louder, and the older and taller boy gave him an affectionate little shove. Cocky, sure of himself, pulling slightly at his cap, still hurling insults back at the Mugger, he came into the dugout. Grouchy spoke as he passed.

"Listen, you fresh young busher, quit needling that guy, will ya? Lay off him, Bob; he's poison. One of these days you'll get yourself hurt."

The boy yanked his bat from the rack. He

started toward the plate. "I'll send you a night letter if anything happens, Grouchy."

The old manager shook his head. He started to reply and checked himself. After all, when you don't say anything you never have to eat your own words.

Through the sixth, the seventh, and the eighth innings they preserved that one-run lead. In the ninth, with victory only three putouts away, they were still leading one to nothing. Then Lefty tired, and a batter got a two-base hit. He was sacrificed to third and the Mugger, swinging his great club, came angrily to the plate.

Grouchy at once signaled from the bench and he was passed. Now the Mugger was really angry. Cut down stealing, nailed by that doubleplay in the fourth, he had struck out in the seventh and was passed in the ninth. Three for nothing! That meant both those boys would pass him in the batting averages. So the Mugger was angry. Especially as he was the man the scouts had come to watch. Everyone knew there were scouts in the stands that afternoon to see whether he was ready for the big time.

He stood on first, hitching up his belt and glaring over at the young second baseman, while the crowd roared. One out, men on first and third, and the Volunteers one run ahead. A hit might mean the game. It could mean the pennant and the Dixie Series.

Then the batter swung, and even with the swing Spike, the shortstop, knew the ball was his. A clean grasscutter, fast and easy to handle, a doubleplay ball just where he wanted it. One toss, one throw, and bang! There you are back in the dugout and the game over. Bob stood waiting on second as the Mugger roared wildly down the basepath and came riding in with his spikes glistening in the late afternoon sun. There was a screen of dust, the sound of body contact, the ripping noise of spikes, and Bob was rolling in the dirt behind the bag.

"Hey! You can't do that, Mugger! You can't rough up my brother. When you rough up my brother, you rough up me!"

The Mugger slapped the dust and dirt from his pants. He stood on the bag, his lips snarling. "I can't, can't I? Consider yourself roughed, young fella."

There was no ballpark, no game. There was no large crowd, no Dixie Series waiting for the winner. Nothing but his brother in agony on the basepath and the Mugger standing contemptuously on the bag. So Spike cranked up his

Sunday punch and let fly. The Mugger went down, head over heels in the dirt.

Confusion! The Crackers were swarming out of their dugout and his teammates were holding Spike back and Grouchy came running up. Soon everyone was involved in the battle. Fans ran onto the field, and it was half an hour before they were cleared off and the two teams separated. By this time Bob had been carried in to the dressing room, a substitute came in to play second, and the game was resumed.

All the time Spike was thinking not of the fight nor the game but of his brother. Gosh, if he's really banged up, I'll finish the Mugger. So help me, I will.

The next batter popped out and a minute later the inning ended with the score one to one. They came in, hot and panting, to the bench.

"Hey, how is he? How is he, Grouchy?"

"Him?" There was scorn in Grouchy's tone. "He's O.K. Torn his legs a little, that's all. You young fool, why you wanna do a thing like that? You like to get yourself benched for a week right now when we need you bad. You'll get a good stiff fine slapped on you as it is. Go in there and play ball. Get me back that run, you young hothead."

Knowing his brother was all right, Spike went up to the plate loose and easy. Not even the realization that the Cracker pitcher would be throwing at his head bothered him.

Just so the kid isn't hurt, that's all that counts. Pennants, Dixie Series, sure. But we depend on each other; he depends out there on me and I depend on him.

As he expected, the first pitch flattened him. He sprawled in the dust, not angry, amused. Slowly he picked himself up.

O.K., big boy, lemme see another one of those high pitches. You oughta remember what I did to one of those in Atlanta last month. That's what I get paid for hitting, mister, that pitch. I love it.

It wasn't another duster. The pitcher pulled the string on him. It was a floater, slow, tantalizing. He was cool now, and waited. Here it comes!

The right field fence in Nashville is one of the shortest in the game. The ball struck a big warehouse across the street and bounced back into the midst of a crowd of boys on the opposite curbing. Inside the park the fans rose yelling. This was what they'd come for, this was it, a ninth inning homer in a crucial game. Now the Vols were ahead by three games. Before Spike had reached second, hats were being passed round in the stands. In Nashville, like many minor league towns, the fans know how to show appreciation, and Spike would get an extra hundred dollars for that homer which won the game. He wasn't interested. He was galloping past the bags, hurrying to reach the bench and the locker room.

At the door he saw Bob lying naked on the table. Bloody clothes were on the floor, and the Doc was snipping away at the plaster about his legs and thighs. Spike stood in the doorway a second, looking at the slim figure, and something brought back a scene that had happened years before. The Old Lady was alive, keeping that dreary boarding-house on West Forrest. One night after dinner when they'd helped wash the dishes, she took them on the street cars to Marbridge, front seat all the way there and back. When they got off at the corner nearest home, the popcorn man was there, his gaslight flickering in the darkness.

Hey, Ma! Can we have some popcorn, can we?

About the stand were half a dozen kids from the Richman gang. But the popcorn wasn't ready and the Old Lady had to return. Bob said he'd wait, so she gave him ten cents for two bags.

All the time Spike had known he shouldn't go off and leave Bob standing there alone with the gang. They reached home and he didn't come and he didn't come. Then he came. He came crying, with blood over his face and arms, and two torn bags with only a fistful of popcorn.

The memory of that evening came back to Spike as he stood in the doorway and saw his brother stretched out on the rubbing table, his thighs patched with surgeon's plaster. Then the others came up behind, pushing him inside, and Bob on the table looked up and saw him. His eyes shining with pride, he reached with both arms for the shoulder of his elder brother.

"Boy . . . I bet you could lick Joe Louis."

He meant it, too.

2

They sat together in the hotel room, Grouchy in the easy chair under the lamp, Ted Fuller, the Dodger scout, facing him. Fuller was talking.

"As you see 'em, Grouchy, just what's different about these boys? What makes 'em tick?"

"Well, for one thing, those two kids can do everything around the bag and do it faster and with more sureness than any pair I've ever seen."

"Yeah! What've they got?"

"Dunno. Mebbe it's the way they get rid of the ball. You musta noticed it when you was here last spring. You musta seen it out there this afternoon on that doubleplay ball in the fourth. It's bang, bang, bang, every play. No sooner get their hands on the ball, than flash!—they get rid of it. Seems like they have that split-second quickness you need for doubleplays. A few players just naturally have it but not many."

"No, that's right. Not many. They're plenty fast, all right."

"Fast! Why, they're acrobats, that's what they are. They make plays you wouldn't believe."

"Would you say, now, Grouchy, would you say they're the best doubleplay combination in this league?"

"The best?" He sat up in his chair. "The best in the league? Look here, Ted, I'll tell you what. I'll say they're the best doubleplay combination I've seen for many years."

"Well, I'll admit you've seen plenty. This kid at short covers ground pretty good."

"And he'll improve, too. Spike's tall but he isn't filled out yet. Give him another season, wait until . . ."

The telephone rang. "Here he is now. Yes? O.K. Send him up. Now then, Ted, you'll see what I mean when I say he's a cool customer. He's good and he knows he's good, and he won't mind saying so, either. Y'see they're orphans, and this one acts as business manager for 'em."

They sat for a minute or two in silence. Then there was a knock.

Spike wore a faded sports coat with a kind of leather patch over each sleeve where his elbows had begun to come through. His sleeves were too short, his trousers were baggy and hardly reached his shoes. But, unlike many tall boys, he had no gawkiness in his movements as he came easily into the room.

"G'd evening, Mr. Devine." It was Grouchy on the bench and in the ballpark, but it was Mr. Devine in his room at the Andrew Jackson. Besides, he was due for a dressing-down over the afternoon's incident, and he knew the manager didn't like familiarity at such moments.

Then he saw the stranger.

"Ted, this is Spike Russell, our shortstop. Spike, shake hands with Ted Fuller of the Dodgers."

Ted Fuller, the Dodger scout! They were going to ask him first-off about the Mugger. Things get around a ballclub fast, and everyone knew there were scouts in the stands that afternoon. I must be careful what I say, he thought.

"Yessir. Glad to see you, Mr. Fuller."

"Sit down, Spike, sit down. I've been watching you out there some time now. You boys handle that ball nicely."

"Yessir, thank you, Mr. Fuller. Me and Bob been playing together quite a while."

"You sure manage to get that ball off fast, Spike. How many doubleplays you think you've made this year?"

Should he tell him or shouldn't he? Was there a catch to that question? Well, here goes. "A hundred and seven so far this year, sir. We led the league last season with a hundred and thirty-two. It's basketball, you see."

"Basketball?"

"Yessir. We both played basketball lots back home in Charlotte when we were kids. All that quick handling and passing, the pivoting and so forth, helps a man in this game."

"I can see it does. Never thought of that. Suppose you're right. You like basketball better than baseball?"

"Nosir, no, Mr. Fuller. We like baseball." When was he going to get down to business, to the Mugger and his chances? If a call-down was due, he wanted it over and done with.

"Tell me about yourself, Spike. You and Bob now, how long you been at it?"

"Why, 'bout six-seven years. We played together quite some time. Started in the Tobacco League in Carolina. Then we jumped outlaw ball and got us a job on the Greenwood team down Mississippi way."

"Greenwood? Oh, yes, that used to be a Giant farm. Where'd you go from there?"

"To Savannah, sir."

"The Sally League! D'ja like it?"

"Yessir. 'Cept it's awful doggone hot there. Why, sir, you wouldn't believe it, come August the flies and bugs are so thick you can't hardly see the ball in the air at night. They come round in the bleachers and spray the fans with Flit for ten cents; but they don't ever spray the players."

"Ha! That's a good one, Grouchy. Spraying the fans with Flit for a dime. I never heard that before. What then? Where'd you go from there?"

"Why, we got a chance with the Dallas Rebels. Next year we managed to hitch up as utility outfielders with the Little Rock Travelers, and the year after that they put us in the infield. Then we come on here with Grouchy."

He paused and looked closely at the stranger. The visitor wore an expensively cut, beige-colored suit, and a handsome necktie. He seemed immaculate and dressy beside Grouchy, sprawled in the easy chair in shirtsleeves and slippers.

"Spike! How'd you like to come up to the Dodgers?"

A fan whirred on the wall. Otherwise silence hung over the room.

"You want us to come up to the Dodgers? Right now?" There was anxiety in his tone and firmness also.

"We want *you* to come up."

"You mean I should leave Bob, Mr. Fuller?" Was that what the man was saying? Leave Bob, the best guy that ever lived, and go up there alone to that club? Not a chance!

The other was laughing. He shot a glance at Grouchy. Then he laughed some more. It was a pleasant, agreeable laugh, a laugh that said: I know. I am used to dealing with folks, to getting along with people.

"Well now . . . maybe . . . we could even find a place for Bob, too."

"Gee!" The anxiety left his voice and the heaviness dropped from his heart. Imagine! Exchanging twelve hundred dollars for three thousand a year. "Gee! That'd be fine. But look, you don't mean to tell me the Dodgers are getting rid of guys like Ginger Crane and Eddie Davis?"

The stranger passed his hand over his forehead. "I don't know what's in their minds up there. I haven't any idea what they plan on, Spike. They don't let me in on their confidence. It's a very different outfit from what it was under Dave Leonard; it's run differently since he went to the Browns. All I know is I had orders to check on you boys again and see whether you were ready for the big time. Grouchy says you are. I guess I'd have to agree. How they'll play you, or where, I don't pretend to know. Ginger Crane isn't the man he was around short five years ago for the Cubs. No secret about that. He can't take it any more when the diamonds get hard and sun-baked toward the end of the season. His legs are going. Then there's Street on third; well . . . they'll work it out some way, I guess. When do you think you could get off?"

"You mean to go . . . to leave . . . to go North?"

"That's what I mean."

Leave Nashville! Go North! It was almost like leaving home. Leave all the boys and old Grouchy; why, Grouchy wasn't a bad guy if you worked. He didn't stand for any loafing, but he wasn't a bad guy. Grouchy could have insisted on keeping them there all summer. And the fans, too. The fans who were your friends, the fans who followed you every night, who shelled out when you hit a homer for them in a crucial game. Exchange all that for a possible berth on the Dodgers. Just the idea sort of took your breath away.

The stranger was talking. "Where's your stuff, Spike? Where you boys live?"

"Out to the boarding-house, Mr. Fuller. It's Mis' Hampton's boarding-house on McGavock Street."

"Think you could get out there in a taxi and grab your stuff and be ready to take the midnight plane from the airport? If I could get you reservations, that is?"

The midnight plane for New York! Half an hour ago he was coming into the room to get a dressing-down from old Grouchy and maybe hear how much of a fine would be slapped on. Now they were talking about the midnight plane for New York!

Hey, Bob! Hey, Bobby! We're going up to the Dodgers!

3

Spike looked over at Bob and Bob glanced back quickly at Spike, both thinking the same thing. Last night this time we were eating supper in Mrs. Hampton's boarding-house on McGavock Street in Belmont Heights, Nashville. Now here we are dashing across Brooklyn Bridge in a limousine with the Dodgers, while up ahead a siren blares and snorts. That's the police escort. Seems like in this league the top teams get a police escort when they have to make a train at the station.

Nashville to Brooklyn. Why, it was only one day, yet a day containing a thousand hours. Surely it was a thousand hours since that supper in Nashville. First of all the long plane ride over a dozen cities, clusters of twinkling lights far below, while everyone dozed save Spike and Bob, far too excited for sleep. Then the descent into the airport at La Guardia Field in New York, with the sun rising on the horizon. A tall man who introduced himself as Bill Hanson, the club secretary, had met them there. Then breakfast at the hotel—fruit juice and cereal, coffee and eggs and bacon, wheat cakes, too, all you could eat. Next the ballpark, with the players arriving for the day's doubleheader against the Giants, and Ginger Crane, the shortstop and manager, famous throughout baseball, who entered looking more like a Broadway actor or a business executive than a ballplayer. Finally the Dodger monkey suits, and the practice for a couple of hours with dozens of photographers taking their pictures, and Bob out there making one of those impossible single-handed stabs. Last of all, the doubleheader they had watched from the bench.

All this in twenty-four hours. No, in a thousand hours. Now they were the Russell boys of the Dodgers, leaving with the team to make the last western trip of the season. It was ages since they'd sat together in Mrs. Hampton's boarding-house on McGavock Street where the stew for supper was gone whenever the game lasted more than nine innings. A thousand hours had passed since then.

The station in New York was a cavern, not a station. It was bigger far than anything they could imagine, yet jammed with Sunday evening travelers. In the confusion they became separated from the team. Some bad moments followed. Whichever way they looked were strange faces, everywhere strange faces, people hurrying for trains or from trains, no one they had ever seen.

Say! Suppose we lost the club for good, suppose we missed that train! Why, we'd get shot back to Nashville pronto.

Silently they wandered through big dome-shaped areas, into waiting rooms, edging through the crowd into telephone rooms, baggage rooms, searching vainly for someone they recognized. No team anywhere! Finally Spike went up to a stationmaster in uniform. The official looked at them curiously but there was no excitement in his voice.

"The Dodgers? You boys with the Dodgers? They're doing all right these days, aren't they?" Slowly he drew a long black-covered book from his coat pocket and consulted it. "I think they're on 24. That's right. They're on the American, platform 24, over there. Don't go down the main entrance where that crowd is. Go over opposite; the ballclubs go down the back way."

Spike saw them then across the crowded space as they went over. The tanned, self-assured athletes were surrounded by a dozen women. Many of the players were dressed in silk sports shirts, open at the neck, and slacks; they wore no coats and had no baggage. Spike and Bob felt strangely out of place in their best suits with neckties on, and bags in their hands. Spike recognized one or two of the men: Razzle Nugent, the tall pitcher, and the swarthy outfielder, Karl Case, and Crane, the manager. Finally they discovered the secretary. He glanced at a slip of paper in his hand.

"Here you are! The Russell boys . . . you boys are H in FB-2." He turned away.

Now what did that mean?

"Beg your pardon, sir."

"H in FB-2. Room H in car FB-2. Go down those steps, right here . . ."

"Sir, how 'bout the tickets? We ain't got our tickets yet."

He smiled. "You boys won't need any tickets.

Just hop aboard. I'll take care of everything."
They walked down the steps to a platform with a long train beside it. Halfway down was a pile of baggage, rows of expensive leather suitcases and handbags, the pile guarded by an elderly man who might have been a banker. He knew them even if they didn't know him.

"Hullo there, boys. You're in FB-2. Up the end of the platform. That all the stuff you got with you? I wish the others traveled light, too."

"Yessir, thank you, sir." Spike then recognized him as the locker room attendant who had fitted them out with their monkey suits, a man the players all addressed as Chiselbeak. For a second he wished they had something more than their two cloth handbags, but after all those were plenty for their needs. They walked down the train. A conductor stopped them.

"Tickets, please. The cars are not ready yet."

"We're with the Dodgers. Room H in car FB-2."

The conductor immediately nodded respectfully and pointed ahead. Astonishing how the password worked. At last they found a window of one Pullman with the figures FB-2.

The conductor standing at the entrance greeted them with deference and the porter took their bags and ushered them inside. A draught of cool air swept their faces, clean and refreshing after the intense August heat of the station. They were walking on a thick carpet through a passageway into the car. It was new, painted a delicate green, with soft indirect lighting overhead. Down the side by the windows was a long corridor from which opened a dozen doors. The porter pushed theirs open. It was like nothing they had ever seen; a small room, compact and complete in every detail. On the side opposite the corridor was a wide plush seat.

"Yeah, O.K. But where'm I gonna sleep?" interjected Bob.

The porter grinned. "You boys making your first trip with the club? Where you-all from? Where? Nashville? Sure 'nuff! That's mah home town, yessir. See, we let this down, the upper one, like this." He stepped up and, reaching above with a kind of key in his hand, released the upper berth which dropped down. He stood hesitating. Spike instantly guessed what he wanted and fumbled for a dime. The porter hesitated no longer. He left abruptly. While Spike stood thinking: This trip is going to cost money, a dime here, a dime there . . .

Now the players were pouring in, followed by

porters staggering under the luxurious leather suitcases and bags. They entered their rooms, banging doors, calling to each other up and down the corridor, the loud, cheerful sounds of healthy men off duty. They were happy after winning the afternoon's doubleheader and pulling up within two games of the league-leading Pirates. Their voices echoed up and down the car, evidently filled with ballplayers. Strange faces passed by the room, glanced at the two boys and went on. Sitting stiffly on the edge of the plush seat, they heard the strange voices and felt like homesick boys at a new school. All that banter was something in which they had no part.

"Hey, Jake, how 'bout a game after dinner. . . . Yeah, I played Terre Haute one season. They call it Terrible Hot out there and, b'lieve me, it *is* hot . . . I was round the course in 82; yes I was, too. You ask Karl . . . Hey, guys, c'mon! I could eat a raw potato . . . Who's for dinner . . . ."

Spike realized he was hungry. A sandwich would surely taste good. Then a figure brushed past, someone with a round frank face and open brown eyes who looked in at them curiously. He hesitated a minute and half smiled. Spike immediately recognized him. Bob didn't.

"Who's that?"

"Sssh. Not so loud, Bob. That must be Tucker, the boy who led the league in batting a few years ago." The figure passed by once more and Spike hailed him.

"Say, Mister, is there any place here we could get us a sandwich?"

"You're the Russell boys from Nashville, aren't you? Heard all sorts of good things about you boys. I'm Roy Tucker." He entered and shook hands with them. "Our dining car is up front three-four cars. We've also got our own lounge car, too; that's the one beyond the diner. Say, lemme know if I can help any. I only came up myself a few years ago."

They looked at each other. Private diners, private lounge cars. Boy, is this a life!

"Let's go, Bobby."

They went out and moved toward the front of the car, pulling and tugging on the door until they discovered that the handle pulled sideways instead of directly backward. From the platform of the car they noticed several players saying good-by to elegant ladies beside the train. Porters with more baggage shoved past. Then the next car, another softly lighted interior, and the next. Spike read the names as they passed,

Boerlikon, Carlton Club, Wiscasset, Lorna Doone, Loch Lomond. At last the diner, even more elaborate than the sleeping cars. They were dazzled for a second by the white table-cloths, the silver, and the pink lamps on every table.

The waiter seated them and handed each one a menu. "Anything to drink?" asked the chief attendant, dressed in a uniform like a rear admiral. They both shook their heads and then began to study the menu, as long a menu as they had ever seen.

Bob glanced across the table at Spike. What prices, his eyes said. Nothing to eat for less than a dollar seventy! Why, we'll be bankrupt if we have to eat in Pullmans.

Other players sauntered in, sat down, and ordered with a casual air. Spike noticed large steaks brought to them, and some drank beer with their dinners, meals that must have been even more expensive than their own. Spike and Bob ate silently and quickly. Then the former paid the bill and left a quarter on the table. No, it wasn't a dime here and a dime there, but a dime here and a quarter there.

They went out, eyed by the bored-looking players at the tables in the ornate diner. Loch

Lomond. Lorna Doone. Wiscasset. Carlton Club. Boerlikon. The train seemed never to end. At last they reached their room.

Spike sat down to figure the cost of the meal. Why, it was about what two meals a day for a week cost in Mrs. Hampton's boarding-house in Nashville.

A figure stood in the doorway. "You boys eaten?" It was the secretary. He had a handful of papers in his hand and looked weary.

Spike stood up. "Yessir. We were just out to the diner."

"Good! The newspaper boys want a story tonight, and I'll bring 'em back a little later most likely."

It was a command. "Yessir. Mr. Hanson, please, now these dining cars, seems like they're mighty expensive. You reckon me and Bob could get us a sandwich or something on these trains?"

Hanson stood rocking back and forth with the motion of the car, not saying anything at all for a minute. Then a grin came over his face. "You don't mean to say you *paid* for your grub?"

"Yessir. Four sixty, counting the tip."

Four sixty! And two meals a day at Mrs. Hampton's boarding-house only cost four bucks fifty a week!

"You shouldn't have done that. You boys have signing privileges. You see, you sign for your meals. Just write your name and Brooklyn Baseball Club on the checks."

"You mean we should order whatever we want from the menu and then write our names down?"

"That's it. I'll try to get you your money back tonight. But in the future you sign for all your meals."

He went on down the car. Bob was fumbling on the wall where a row of gadgets and buttons were placed. "Wonder what some of these things do?" He pushed a button. Far off in the distance was a soft tinkle like the sound of temple bells. Spike had heard it before supper and wondered what it meant. In a few seconds the porter stuck his nose in their doorway.

"You gentlemen call?" Bob's expression was blank. The porter disappeared.

An hour later the secretary was back again. He had half a dozen men at his heels. They filed into the small bedroom, filling it completely until there was no space whatever to stand in, and one or two of them blocked the doorway, looking over each other's shoulders. Strangers, all of them, strangers and more strangers. It was like a kind of secret service examination. If only someone they knew had been there, Grouchy, for instance.

"Spike, shake hands with Jim Foster of the *Times*; you'll see plenty of him before Christmas. And this is Rog Stevens of the *Tribune*, and here's Stan King of the *Telegram* and Tommy Heeney of the *Brooklyn Eagle* and Ed Morgan of the *Sun*. Boys, this is his brother Bob. Bob, meet the boys."

They shook hands all round. They made the two boys dizzy as they eyed them queerly, got out pencils, and began writing on the backs of envelopes or on folded sheets of paper. What did they find to write about?

The Russell boys of the Dodgers. . . .

4

Ginger Crane came into the hotel room with Johnny Cassidy, the third base coach. The manager was dressed in a delicate fawn-colored gabardine cut by an expensive tailor. He threw a newspaper on a table, one of the few tables unoccupied by papers, suitcases of leather with silver fastenings, magazines, and other belongings. The room was large with elaborate furniture, a davenport with a silk brocade covering, heavy armchairs, and fancy tables. Ginger was entirely at home in this luxury. He walked across to an adjoining bath and presently reappeared, wiping his hands on a towel.

"Shoot! We needed that game the worst way. That's a tough one to drop right at this point."

"Can't win 'em all," rejoined the coach philosophically.

The manager was hardly in a philosophical mood. How can you be philosophical when you're the one who carries the team on your shoulders, when you sit out there on the bench and see your men helpless and almost hitless in a critical game against the leaders, when you sweat under a hot September sun as your chances for the lead dwindle and dwindle before your eyes?

"We oughta had that one! The team isn't hitting. When a team isn't hitting, what can you do? Look at Case! Look at Red Allen! Look at Harry Street! I suppose he'll claim he can't hit because he was moved to third! Roy Tucker's the only man who's hitting."

Cassidy sank into an armchair. He tried to be consoling and cool the boss off. The boss hated to lose and of all games this was surely a tough one to drop. "Aw, they're not playing bad baseball, Ginger. They're playing good ball, only they're facing hot pitching. Everywhere we go we have to meet the hot ones. That's why they aren't hitting."

"Shoot! When a team has no pep, when they just play all-right baseball and nothing more, well, what then? What you gonna do?" He sank into an easy chair himself. "We should have had that game. Leaving New York last week we were only two games behind. Now look; we're three and a half!"

"Well, we still got a month, haven't we?"

"A month! A month! Six months wouldn't do if we don't start to hit. It's enough to make a guy nuts when you consider a train wreck is better than a nice, sunshiny afternoon."

Was the boss really getting the jitters? Cassidy looked up. "How do you figure that one?"

"Why, in a train wreck a man at least has an even chance of getting out alive. But baseball always hits a team in its most vulnerable spots. We went into that tailspin on that sunny day in Boston when Swanny and I both picked up charleyhorses the same afternoon. Train wreck, my eye! We wouldn't have lost both of us at the same time!"

Cassidy tried to change the subject from gloomy things. "Well, I like this boy out there at short. The more I see of him the better I like him. He'll do. That was a smart move, Ginger."

Cassidy flipped open a newspaper and turned

to the sports pages. He reached up to pull on the light of a lamp over his shoulder. It didn't go on. He yanked again with no result. This was sufficient to set off the explosion. Ginger jumped from his chair for the telephone.

"Manager!" There was anger in his voice and on his face the same hard, cruel look as when he edged up to umpires in a close game, his jaw out, stuck up to theirs. "Hey, Clarkson! This is Crane talking. How about fixing the light in this room, in the big room to my suite?"

There was a reply, the usual reply.

Ginger immediately went to work. "Now, look, that's the old runaround, the same old runaround, see, and I'm sick and tired of it. I don't want any more of it. I spoke to the room clerk last night; nothing doing; I speak to the room clerk this morning; still nothing doing. Never mind what they said . . . I don't care what they told you . . . that's your funeral. If my ballclub doesn't win games, the boss takes it out on me, not the players. And I want that light fixed and fixed now, y'understand? This club brings you a good many thousand dollars every summer, and this is not the only hotel in town, nosir; we can go to the Schenley, we can go to the Fort Pitt, we can go to. . . . Never mind that, you get an electrician here and get him right away."

He slammed the phone down. "There, now let's see if we can get a little service around this place."

Cassidy in the meanwhile, used to the explosions of his boss, had changed quietly over to another chair where the light functioned, and was reading the sports pages. "Hey, listen, Ginger! Here's what Foster says about this Russell boy. 'He wasn't very impressive the first night out from New York as he sat in a drawing room on the train with his kid brother and "mistered" the baseball writers. But as soon as Spike put on his monkey suit and started working at short, you didn't have to look long to realize the Dodgers had a find. Tall and lanky and quick, he's as fast or faster getting back for the short ones as anyone in the league.' "

The manager only half listened. He wasn't really interested in sports writers or in the two Russell boys, either. He was interested in Ginger Crane's troubles, especially his losing ballclub. "He may do, he may do. Tell you, John, I'll shake up this club and every man on it until I find a winning combination."

"D'ja notice him this afternoon in the fifth? Is

that kid fast!" continued Cassidy. "You should have heard him rave over in Cinci that night when he came out on the field and saw real lights for the first time. Took one look around. 'Wow!' he says. 'What lights!' "

"Yeah," replied the manager absent-mindedly. "There just aren't any good lights in the minors. And the lower you get, the worse they are, too. Heck, where's that electrician?"

"The kid was telling me he was playing in the Sally League or somewhere down South where they had a light pole behind the plate, one on the right field foul line, and one on the left field line. Center field was black. One night the center fielder brought a flashlight out on the field, and the umpire threw him out of the game for kidding."

"Yeah . . . I don't doubt . . . I wouldn't wonder in the least." The manager was walking nervously up and down the room. "Where's that dad-ratted electrician . . ."

"Personally, I hardly blame the boy, myself. I've seen some of these bush league plants, and I want to tell you I've got more light in my bathroom to shave by than they have to play ball with."

"Where's that electrician?" stormed Ginger.

The team's failure to catch up on the leaders was telling; he was nervous and only able to show his nerves alone in his suite with someone like the coach around. "Shoot! How long's it take for them . . ."

There was a timid knock at the door. The manager with his quick reaction was there in two steps and flung it open. Outside stood a panting boy in a faded pair of trousers, a tired-looking polo shirt, and old shoes well worn at the toes. In short, a typical hotel employee. "You an electrician?" He glared at the hatless boy.

"Why . . . yessir. That is, I worked as an electrician . . ."

"O.K. C'mon in. Don't stand there yawping. C'mon in and fix my light. I'm sick and tired of asking you people to do things and never having them done. Now get busy and no backtalk."

The boy entered cautiously. He looked at the light socket. Then he changed bulbs with no result, and next produced an ancient penknife from his pocket and unscrewed the lamp socket. His movements were quick and capable; his manner had lost its timidity; he was an expert now and the two high-priced ballplayers watching were useless dunderers of no help in this particular crisis. He forgot them. Untwisting a wire, he cut away some sheathing, cut the rubber tubing from it, tinkered a minute at the wire with a blade from his penknife, rewound it again. With a screwdriver attached to the knife he replaced the socket and screwed it in, placed a bulb in it, pulled the chain. The light went on.

"There you are, sir."

"O.K. Thanks. It's about time."

"Yessir. Now, sir, please can I . . ." He was standing by the door, holding the handle for support.

"No! Get out! Get out, d'you hear me?" No longer was Ginger the useless dunderer in matters electrical; he was the twenty-five-thousand-dollar manager of the Dodgers with a faltering ballclub on his shoulders. "Get out! That's all, just get out." He went over and slammed the door.

The coach looked up from his paper across the room. "Seems as if I'd seen that boy somewhere before."

"Yeah. He was sort of familiar, wasn't he?"

Then another knock came on the door, not a timid respectful one, either. A man stood outside in overalls, with screwdrivers and other tools in little patch pockets of the trousers.

"You gotta light here needs fixing?"

For once the manager was speechless. "Why, no. He fixed it for us."

"Who fixed it?" The hour was late, the night was hot, and he had just received a call-down from the manager, so he was in no pleasant mood. To a hotel electrician the boss of the Dodgers was not a twenty-five-thousand-dollar big shot, but simply the cranky gent in 1016 who was causing all the trouble.

"The electrician. He only just came up here."

"What is this, anyway? I'm the electrician."

"I'm telling you the electrician was just here and fixed our light."

"Say, mister, I'm not for no jokes tonight. I got work to do. Show me your light needs fixing, will ya?"

"Whatsa matter with you? I told you the electrician just came, didn't I?" Cassidy looked up from his chair. He had a feeling that with two edgy tempers in one room, somebody was due for trouble, and he hoped not to be in on it. Then the telephone rang.

"Yeah!" Ginger's voice was sharp and raspy. "Who? Who? Oh, you . . . it was who . . . it was you . . . you did . . . you fresh young busher, why didn't you . . . I did *so* give you a chance to open your trap . . . why, we both thought, we both figured you were the hotel electrician . . . I see . . . I see. Well, you rockhead, you certainly know your stuff. I only hope you'll be as good out there on the field as you were . . . yeah . . . he just came up . . . you wanted what? To ask a question? O.K., shoot!"

There was silence for a moment or two and then the manager's irritation vanished. His mood changed, his face softened, his mouth wrinkled up, and he began to grin. He nodded his head. Then he put his hand over the mouthpiece of the telephone, threw back his head and laughed.

At last he got control of himself. "Yeah. That's right. That's it. You guessed it. Some of the boys, well now, they think it's funny to pull those things on you fellows up from the minors. O.K. O.K., and thanks for fixing the light. What's that? Yes, I will. Yep, I'll use you as soon as I find the right spot. O.K., boy, so long!"

"Well!" The coach and the electrician, still standing by the door with an angry look on his face, stared at him. "Say! I've heard of some queer ones before, but this rockhead takes the bun. You know who our electrician was, Johnny?"

"Sure. It was young Russell, Spike Russell's brother, the kid."

"For Pete's sake, why didn't you tell me?"

"I only realized it myself while you were talking there." The manager addressed the electrician. "Mac, I'm sorry about all this. That kid I was talking to just now is a rookie on the team and only been with us a few days. When he knocked, I figured he was the electrician I'd been hollering for. Seems the boy works winters in his home town as an electrician, so he knew just what to do." He turned to the coach. "Johnny, here's one for the book. This kid came up to ask what he should do. His room's on the 18th floor, and someone tells him that in these big city hotels they charge ten cents every time you take the express elevator above the twelfth floor. So for the last three days the kids have been getting off at the twelfth and walking six flights to save a dime!"

5

From the bleachers in deep center, from the stands back of the plate, from both sides came the sounds of baseball, the familiar sounds and noises to which Spike and Bob were accustomed, those same metallic voices to be heard in every park in every city of the league.

"Cain't tell the players without a score-card . . . peanuts . . . fresh roasted peanuts . . . get 'em ice cold . . . ice cold tonic . . . you cain't tell the players . . ."

The noises were more than familiar; they were consoling and reassuring to the two youngsters taking fielding practice before the game, Bob at second while Ed Davis was having a sore muscle in his leg limbered up by the trainer.

In the front seat of a box sat Jack MacManus, the owner of the club, and leaning against the rail talking to him was Cassidy, the coach.

"You know, that boy reminds me of Bill Jackson; yes, he does. He's got the same hands and the same stream-lined legs; notice, they aren't the knotty kind, they're built for speed. I hit to him in fielding practice yesterday, and he was out there yelling at me, 'What's the matter? Why don't you give me a tough one?' He's a sweetheart, all right."

Together the men watched the two youngsters cavorting on the grass under the hot sun. The diamond was hard and fast, and one could see they both enjoyed themselves. Now they were together they were pepper and salt, grabbing balls from every position, flipping them across to each other in a familiar manner, burning them to first or third. All the while Bob kept up that flow of chatter and comment which never ceased when he was in action; which was so much a part of his play he seldom realized he was talking. They forgot the enormous two-decked stands, forgot even that they were under constant inspection by every eye on the club. They were not a couple of rookies trying to break into big-league baseball. They were two frisky kids having themselves a good time in the steaming sun. Then the cocky youngster behind second shouted at the man at the plate who was hitting to them. He made a quick motion with his bat, and cracked a sizzling liner over the pitcher's box. It hit the dirt in front of second.

The two boys were off together. Both were near the ball, on top of it almost, so fast that either could have stabbed for it. But Bob suddenly realized his brother was the one to make the play, and as he neared the bag sheered away to clear the path for the throw. Spike picked up the ball a few feet from the base, and in one continuous motion touched the bag and hurled the ball to first in time to nab the fastest runner in baseball. Only an expert could have felt their understanding, their coordination as they made that decision in the fraction of a second when the ball roared toward them. The two men in the box behind the dugout missed nothing. They looked at each other. Base hits, they knew, were a matter of feet. Doubleplays were a matter of inches.

Half an hour later, with Ed Davis playing at second, Spike felt anything but coordinated. The veteran was knowledgeable and steady, he seldom made errors. Also, Spike noticed, he seldom tried for impossible balls, especially those to his right, the hard side. Moreover, he was slow starting. To Spike, used to his brother's timing and his brother's agile movements, the old-timer often seemed anchored to the ground. It makes a difference in a keystone combination to be with a man you know.

The play came, as those plays invariably do, at a critical moment in a tight game. It was one of those plays when the correct throw means the difference between a run or a put-out, the difference between victory or defeat. A man was on first when the batter hit a stinging grounder to the right of second base. As pivot man, Spike started running for second base when the ball met the bat, watching the veteran go after it. But he was slow, slow. He tried desperately, stabbed it and managed to hold it. Davis, however, threw a hard ball, and Spike was used to Bob's soft ball. In his excitement and eagerness, in his anxiety over the veteran's delay, he forgot this. With an instinctive desire to be in motion for the throw to first, he caught the ball and over-ran the bag, thus failing to make the force-out at second. The runner slid under him safely and later scored with the only run of the game.

By the day the team returned to New York

Spike felt surer of himself; he was more used to Davis and his timing. By then, however, the team was in a hitting slump. Moreover, they were making mistakes you wouldn't believe. Spike and Bob, trained under a disciplinarian, were amazed by the bobbles of some of these big leaguers, made either through tightness, fatigue, or carelessness. Once a hit that wasn't run out, in the next game a throw a fraction of a second late or a fraction of a foot wide, in the next a sloppy play which later resulted in the winning run; these things astounded the Russell boys. So they weren't surprised when the team got back from the West to find they were four games out of first instead of two.

On the whole, Spike felt satisfied with his own game. He was not playing his best because he wasn't playing with his brother; but well enough, and he was hitting almost .300, not bad for his first look at big-league pitching. But the rest of the team, save old reliable Roy Tucker who was always to be depended upon, were not hitting.

Clack-clack, clackety-clack they trooped into the dressing room after losing a tight game behind the four-hit pitching of Razzle Nugent. Disappointed, they sat around glumly. As usual

Raz was on his bench before his locker with the clubhouse boy untieing his shoes.

"O.K. O.K., take 'em off. You want I should go into the showers with my shoes on? I don't wonder you think so, though. They's guys dumb enough on this-here-now club to do it." He glared round the room.

"Tough luck, Razzle." Cassidy, the coach, went past, dragging the leather bat bag after him.

"Yeah! Well, the hawks have got us, I guess. No use. . . ." He threw off his clothes and lumbered into the showers, muttering. When the hawks get you, everything goes wrong. You look for a fastball and get a curve; you look for a hook and you're fooled by a hopping sinker. You mess up easy balls in the field. When the hawks have got you, there isn't much to say.

Most of the players were hurrying into their street clothes, and when Raz finally came out there were only a handful left about the lockers. Razzle turned to Spike who dressed near him. "D'ja see Case on that fly in the eighth? He ran like a mob dispersing."

Spike hardly knew what to say. On teams he had played with before no one criticized a teammate openly. On those teams there had been no Razzle Nugent, either.

"I must be a saint or I'd 'a' choked him to death." He lit a cigarette. "I'm gonna write my wife tonight."

"D'you write your wife every day, Razzle?" It was all Spike could think of to say, for he saw no special connection between Karl Case missing a blooper in left and Razzle's wife. Razzle saw the connection.

"Nope. Not often, not every day. I'm gonna write her tonight, though, and ask her to pack up and come on to New York. If Case can play ball in the big leagues, so can she."

A sportswriter passed across the room from the manager's quarters, hurrying to the door.

"Hey there, Stanley," shouted Razzle. "Wait a sec. Do me a favor, will ya?"

"Whazzat, big boy? Quit writing baseball?"

"Naw! That would be a double favor. I only asked for one. Put in the paper that Case is a semi-pro. The people deserve to know the truth."

There were titters throughout the room from the stragglers dressing, for Case, known in the league as a man who thought chiefly of himself and his batting average, was by no means popular on the club. The sportswriter waved and went out.

Razzle continued dressing, watched closely by the Russell boys and especially by Bob. Bob enjoyed watching Raz garb himself. It was known all over the circuit that Razzle had sixteen suits with accessories to match, and that particular evening he was a scenic effect worth seeing. He put on a gray silk sports shirt, gray silk socks, gray shoes and a gray suit. Then with care he tied and re-tied an elaborate gray silk necktie. He stood five minutes before the mirror brushing his long black hair.

"Well, I'm gonna have me a good time this evening. By gosh. I think I earned it. Four hits I hold 'em down to, and what do I get out of it— a shutout. I'm gonna have me a good time tonight. I'm gonna hire a plane at La Guardia Field and take a ride. Anyone wanna go with me? Wanna go 'long, Spike?"

"Gee, Raz, I'd sure like to. I didn't realize you were an aviator!" Spike looked at the big chap with new admiration. Why, the guy was a wonder. He could do anything.

"I ain't," said Razzle with decision. "Look, this-here-now Case ain't no ballplayer, but he plays ball, don't he? I ain't an aviator, either, so why shouldn't I drive a plane?"

The great man glanced round with scorn and, as no one challenged him, stalked out to a taxi.

Roy Tucker was yanking on his coat. "That guy's a card. They say he has a hundred and fifty-nine neckties, all different, too."

"A hundred and fifty-nine neckties!" said Bob. "Man, what on earth for? What does he want a hundred and fifty-nine neckties for? He's only got one neck, hasn't he?"

6

Under the relentless drive that was keeping the Pirates on top, even some of Ginger Crane's assurance vanished. The hawks really had them, and when the hawks have you nothing goes right and there isn't much you can do. Ginger sat disgustedly in one corner of the bench before the game, talking with Stanley King of the *Telegram*. He hitched his leg up beside him, leaned one arm on his bent knee, and ejected a wad of tobacco onto the sparse grass before the dugout.

"Shoot! Why, when we left on that last western trip in August, when we were two games behind, I'd 'a' bet you all the tea in China we'd come home in front. Now look! Now where are we? Five games back and still slipping."

"I can't yet believe what's happened," he continued. "Last week I just felt we weren't hitting, we were in a slump that couldn't continue. I thought sure we'd get going by this time. But we haven't. Seems like when the hawks have you every break goes the other way. D'ja notice that third strike old Stubblebeard called Sunday on Red with two on base? Things like that hurt."

"You bet. That was a tough one," said the sportswriter sympathetically.

"It slays me. And yesterday that decision on third, against Slugger Case; remember? I didn't get more than an hour's sleep last night, and I guess I look it, too. . . . All right, c'mon now, guys! Wake those bats up there . . ."

That afternoon the team won and everyone felt better. Even winning one game made a difference; the whole attitude of the dressing room changed.

As Spike remarked when he left the park beside Razzle and his brother, "Baseball's a swell game—when you win."

The big pitcher looked solemn. He was having none of that. "No, sir. No, sir," he answered emphatically. "Baseball's a grand game any time."

"You love it, don't you, Razzle?" said Bob.

"I sure do. I eat it. I love to play the game, to talk about it even. If I didn't like it I'd get me another job. See here. If we should win the series, I don't care whether I get a full share or nothing. That's how I feel about baseball. Hullo, bub."

A boy stopped them and asked for their autographs. Spike had observed that some of the team affected to be bored when asked for their signatures, others curtly refused. Not Razzle. He stopped and signed, after which they both signed below him as was proper for a couple of rookies.

The crowd on Montague Street was thinning out. "D'you know how these kids spot ball-players for autographs?" asked Razzle.

"Anyone could spot you a mile off, Raz."

"No, no fooling. They'll spot you, too. Every town they will. Know how they do it?"

They didn't know and Razzle, pleased at the opportunity, explained. He explained simply by pointing to his carefully combed black hair.

"How do you mean?"

"Your hair, see. They notice your hair is wet,

so they know you've been in the showers. O.K., you're a ballplayer. Get it? Simple."

An older boy extended an autograph book and a pen in his hand.

"Sorry to bother you, sorry to be a pest, Mr. Nugent."

Raz paused and signed. "That's all right, bud, I'm not bothered. I like it. The only thing is when folks stop asking me. If people quit pestering me I'll stop eating."

They all signed and passed along. At the parkway Razzle hailed a taxi but the Russells took the subway. Spike, still cautious, was not anxious to spend money needlessly. Back at the hotel, the desk clerk handed them an envelope with their room key.

"It came by special messenger this morning just after you boys left for the park," he said.

The envelope was marked BROOKLYN BASEBALL CLUB on the outside, and was addressed to Mr. Robert Russell. Bob opened it in the elevator and handed it to Spike without a word. It was a short note sending him back to Nashville and enclosing a train ticket with a berth for that evening.

Like that! The unmentionable thing, the thing they never talked about, that they both dreaded, had come. Separation at last. The break-up of the Russell boys, the keystone combination of the Savannah Seals, the Little Rock Travelers, and the Nashville Vols, the boys who had stuck together since their days of outlaw ball in North Carolina, since the time when their mother kept a boarding-house on West Forrest Street, Charlotte. Now at last it had come, the parting, separation, the break-up of the Russell boys. The thing they never talked about and always feared.

"No, sir," said Spike in a definite tone, throwing his coat on the bed. "No, sir! I like it here fine; it's a good bunch of boys and all that, but I won't leave you nohow. And anyway I don't like playing alongside old Davis, really. He chucks a hard ball and I'm used to you throwing a soft one; he don't suit my timing at all; he puts me off more often than not. If you gotta go back, I go back, too."

Bob would have none of this. "Why, man, you must be nuts. What you wanna do, gum our chances for big league ball forever? This guy Davis, he's old; he can't last forever. He's so old he's old enough to be a pitcher."

Despite the soreness inside, Spike laughed.

The age of the pitchers was one of the things

that had most surprised them in the big time. Not that the pitchers weren't good. But they certainly were old, some of them. Bob was right. That man Davis was old; he was nearly through.

"Why, man, you must be plumb crazy. Figure yourself now in Crane's place with the team dropping behind. I saw MacManus come in to the locker room yesterday or the day before and give Ginger Hail Columbia. D'you think Ginger wants to go out there and have the wolves holler at him because he's slow on ground balls or because the team isn't winning? He wants no part of that. He wants to stay right where he is, on the bench. If you quit now he'd never forgive us. And we'd neither of us ever get back into big league ball."

"But to bust us up, to break us up for the first time."

There was a long silence.

"That's baseball, Spike. We've got to do it, we must, so's we can get back together again. Gosh knows, I hate to leave . . ."

To leave. It came over him. To leave it all just as he was getting accustomed to the bigness and the strangeness of everything. To leave the team and the players, who merely looked like base-ball players to the fans in the bleachers but were all his friends now with individual traits: like Fat Stuff's queer, quick steps as he took the mound from the bullpen to relieve in a tight spot, or the beautiful thrashing motion of Razzle's arm when he bore down against a tough batter, and the backhanded stab he always made of the catcher's return. To leave all this, to leave Ebbets Field with the noisy clatter of the vast press box up above, and that sudden "Ooooh!" when a Dodger rapped out a clean hit, and the great crowd on a sunny afternoon looking like a sea of popcorn, and the clack-clack, clackety-clack of spikes on concrete, the smell of the bottles on the stand beside the Doc's rubbing tables, the sound of running water in the showers, the snatches of song when they were winning, and the stations late at night, the cool, empty platform with the sleepers ready and a porter standing beside the steps. To leave the big time and go back to Nashville. Back to the minors, where they traveled in day coaches, where the clubs bought round trip tickets and met in a central city to swap tickets and save money. It hurt to go back to that, but most of all it hurt to go and leave Spike. That's what Bob was thinking as they ate their last cheerless dinner together.

And all the while Spike was thinking: Why, it even helped to have him near, to have him there on the bench, to know he was around. It helped to have him say as they turned in at night, "I wish you were manager of this-here team, Spike." It helped even though it was funny. It helped to listen to that peppery voice in the rallies, that confident cry, "Go get 'em, gang, go get 'em," or his favorite shout when they were batting, "The big one left, boy, the big one left." Those yells, so natural to his ears, sounded almost schoolboyish on this team of veterans who talked about their golf scores, to whom baseball was not excitement and romance but business and nothing else.

Now he'd have another roomie, a strange roomie for the first time in his life, some bored player like Swanson; no one anyway with whom he could feel at home, no one with whom he could discuss the tough plays and the tight moments of the game. While Bob, the best guy who ever lived, the finest little second baseman in all the game, Bob would be back there on the paths for Nashville, living at Mrs. Hampton's boarding-house on McGavock Street in Belmont Heights, and he'd be up here on the Dodgers alone. Completely alone. For the first time.

That's what Spike was thinking as they ate their last cheerless dinner together.

They didn't take long to pack. It doesn't take long to cram a few shirts, a pair of pajamas, and some toilet articles into a small cloth handbag. They were both silently glad they hadn't invested in those expensive leather suitcases with their names in gilt on the end.

Their last time together.

"I think we should take a taxi," suggested Spike, as they went down in the elevator.

"What for? Subway's always got us there, hasn't it?"

Bob was having no sentiment. Neither was anyone else. A couple of players lounging after dinner in the lobby waved an indifferent good-by, Rats Doyle called out to them, and Slugger Case, talking to the newsstand girl, spoke as they passed.

"So long, kid. Don't forget us down there." But he didn't offer to shake hands.

They sure hate to see you leave, thought Bob. Man, that's baseball.

They reached the station. The train was ready. Spike bought a couple of newspapers and handed them to his brother. They both descended to the train. After wandering up and down they finally discovered the car, not a luxurious Pullman divided into separate compartments with indirect lighting and a bell that sounded like a temple in China, but an ordinary sleeper. Bob's ticket called for an upper. He looked at Spike and Spike glanced at Bob, both thinking the same thing. Going back is different from coming up.

The break-up of the Russell boys! Each one was thinking to himself: What a pair we could have been out there around second for the Dodgers. Now we can never show them. How the blazes'll I ever get along without him? Without Spike? Without Bob?

"Say hullo to all the folks at Mis' Hampton's for me. And tell the old dame to be sure and keep some stew for you when there's an extra inning game. No more of that funny stuff. Don't you stand for it, Bob; you gotta get your meals."

"Sure will. I'll tell her."

"And give my regards to Grouchy, the old bear. He taught me lots, tell him."

"You betcha, Spike."

"And all the boys, Tom and Dopey and the rest."

"Yessir. Now you take care of yourself, hear me?"

"You, too. I'll be writing you, Bobby." Writing to Bob, the best guy who ever lived . . .

"Same here. G'd-by."

Why, it had come, now, this minute. The time they never thought would come, ever. It was here at last.

"You'll be back, I reckon, boy."

"You betcha. I'll be back all right."

Yeah, he'll be back. Back on the Cubs or the Cards or the Sox. They can't keep a guy with a pair of hands like that down on the farm very long. But he won't come back to us, though. This is the end, the bust-up of the Russell boys. Here it is. The moment has come, the moment we dreaded, both of us, that we never thought would come, never talked about . . .

He couldn't stand it. He squeezed his brother's hand, turned and walked down the aisle of the car, out of the door. A conductor, watch in hand, was waving slowly to the front of the train.

Then just as Spike stepped onto the platform he was seized by a maniac. The maniac wore no hat, no necktie; he was sweating and excited and very red in the face, different from the way Bill Hanson, the club secretary, usually looked. Usually he was cool, collected, urbane, never upset even when being called down by Jack MacManus, the club owner.

"Hey! Hey, Spike! Get him off, get him off quick . . . your kid brother . . . get him off . . . out . . . off . . . quick . . ."

He ran back along the car toward Bob's seat. At last he found it and began tapping wildly on the window and gesticulating.

"C'mon," he shouted. "Come on out . . . get off . . . get off quick . . . get off, ya bum, ya . . ."

"All aboard! All aboard!" shouted the conductor, snapping his watch just as Bob appeared on the platform of the Pullman, a questioning look on his face. He couldn't understand what it was all about and no more could Spike.

The secretary didn't hesitate. He shoved the conductor aside and, pushing back the porter, grabbed Bob by one arm and hauled him to the platform just as the car began to move.

"Here . . . you can't do that," said the conductor from the car steps.

But Bob was off. The train was moving gently past, the windows filled with passengers, their noses against the glass in an attempt to discover what the excitement and the shouting was about.

"What's up? What's happened, Mr. Hanson?"

"Ed Davis! He caught his bat in the elevator door and it broke his arm. You gotta stay."

"Stay! Stay!" shouted Bob. "I can't . . . "

"You can't? Why not?" Hanson was shrieking now.

"My bag! I left my bag on the train—with all my things."

The secretary stared at him in a fury. Then the anger changed to laughter. "To blazes with your bag! We'll buy you a whole new outfit."

7

Ginger Crane paced up and down the room with nervous steps. His brain trust, Cassidy and Charlie Draper, the two coaches, sat glumly at his side. The boss was in a bad mood, and when the boss was like that suggestions and encouragement were of little help. He walked up and down, up and down, carrying on what he thought was a conversation but what was really a monologue.

"Two months and a half, two months and a half we're in front; two months and a half we have the world by the tail, and then bang! Something hits you. Or you fall down a manhole and everyone cracks you over the head with the lid. First we lose O'Toole, then Greene, and then Davis and . . ."

"D'you think we could . . ." Draper was trying to be helpful, but Crane would have none of it.

"When you're in the spot we're in, you don't think. You're too bewildered to think. You can only feel. After a while everything is a great big headache."

But Draper persisted. "I still think it would help if we could . . ."

"Nothing helps," interrupted the manager. Before the team, on the field or the bench, he had to be confident and cool. In his own room with only his coaches around he could say what he thought, he could really let go, and he was taking advantage of this.

"Nothing helps when you're floundering around the way we are, dropping games left and right. It's strange how helpless a guy feels. Nothing breaks right for you. Sometimes you think you or the world has gone crazy. I swear to heaven, Charlie, I don't know whether to tell the boys to go out and get good and stiff tonight to loosen them up, or ride herd on them harder and harder. I don't know what I should do. I'm so damn tired myself I can't even see straight."

He slumped into a chair. There was a moment of silence over the room.

"Shoot! What have the Pirates got that we haven't got?"

"Only first place," remarked Draper sagely.

For once Crane didn't come back at him as he usually did. To disagree with the peppery manager was usually to bring down a torrent of words on your head.

"Here's how I see things, Ginger." Draper didn't pause between sentences for fear of an interruption. "The team's numb, no use talking. When you came off the field they lost something, a spark if you like . . . well, something in there to fuse 'em. To set 'em moving, to get the rallies started in the tight games. It's the tight ones we've been losing. Now this Spike Russell is a dandy fielder with a fine pair of hands, and he's getting a piece of the ball, too. But he's certainly no sparkplug."

"So what? You want me to go back in there with these feet of mine, and that boy fielding well and hitting over .300?"

"Nope. I want you to let the kid take over."

"The kid. You mean Spike?"

"No, I don't. I mean his brother."

"His brother! The youngster?"

"That's right."

"Why, he's . . . he's . . . I don't believe that boy has started to shave yet. And he's only had four games in the majors since we put him in for Davis last week."

"Makes no never-mind. Take my word for it, he's a natural. That lad's a holler guy. It comes to him naturally, and he isn't scared by these older men, either. Yesterday when Street missed that hit to his left the boy shouts, 'Get off that dime, Harry, get off that dime and move around there.' Then he goes way to his right and makes that one-handed catch of Maguire's liner. Give him the word and he'll go to town."

"Right, Charlie." Cassidy spoke up. "I'd agree to all that. Baseball isn't just a game to this kid, it's life. Why, he's a new person since he got in there. He isn't a pop-off guy like Razzle, but he has that same aggressiveness. He's pepper; it stands out all over him, and he's a mighty tough loser. Believe me, when he gets on base that lad is a spike-flying dervish. I watched him close yesterday."

"Well, we've tried about every combination except pitching the bat-boy, so we might as well try this, too," remarked the manager. "O.K., let's see what he'll do. Come on, boys, time to be moving."

It was just before game time that afternoon when the manager took Bob aside. "Russell, I want you to do something out there from now on. This team needs a punch in the jaw. I want you to be the punch."

Bob was puzzled. "What's that mean? I guess I don't get you."

"From now on you're going to be our holler guy."

"Holler guy?"

"That's it. Holler. Pep. Pepper. Lots of it, too. Don't let the crowds that'll come to see us play the Giants this weekend frighten you. I've got things sized up and, as I see 'em, you're a holler guy. All right, you go out and holler. Give 'em all you got."

He looked at the slender figure in uniform. Maybe, after all, Cassidy is right. Maybe it's a good thing Ed Davis got injured; it'll give me a chance this fall to see what these kids can do, and anyhow we aren't getting any place fast the way it stands now. Since I'm not in there they need pepping up; maybe this boy's youth and freshness will do the trick.

"O.K., sir, if you say so."

"That's it. Let me hear you holler plenty; let me hear you yelling at the infield and the pitcher, too."

"Shucks, the crowd don't scare me; but, gee whiz, do I have to holler at the other fellas on the team who are older and been longer on the club?"

"Yes, you do. Forget the others. Just you holler."

"I will if you want me to. I'll holler if you say the word. But, golly . . . that's some job, that is."

However, no one ever had to tease Bob Russell to "holler." As he remarked that night in their room to his brother, "I can take a hint when a steam roller runs over me." In Nashville despite his youth he had been the "holler guy" of the team, and once out there beside second for the Dodgers, all he needed was a go-ahead from the boss. For he was naturally full of salt, yes, and pepper, too, giving it as well as taking it. His voice echoed daily over the infield. "Go get 'em, gang, le's go get 'em." And his chatter toned up everyone's play.

Moreover, he backed up his voice with deeds. It was Bob's single in the ninth that sent them ahead in the first game of their important series with the Giants. At first some of the older men looked on him as a brash youngster and muttered under their breaths about the "old college try." But his stops and throws around second, his sensational fielding and his work with the stick, forced them to respect this youngster. Gradually they saw that he was more than just a fresh youngster with a strident voice.

Bob made one bad error in the second game against the Giants, dropping a quick throw from the pitcher which would have picked a man off second. The man scored later and the Giants won the game, and for a few days the fans were muttering that the boy certainly booted that one. But in the next game and the game after, which they won, the pair were the Russell boys again.

Spike, tall, lean, was cutting down liners in deep short that a smaller man would never have touched; Bob was darting here and there, like an insect, stopping hot ones behind the bag and then racing out to steal hits between his position and first base. When the big behemoths came roaring down the basepaths, looking as they crashed in like human locomotives, Bob never gave an inch; in fact, he even went out to meet them.

The boys were playing good ball. Of course

they were playing good ball; at last they were happy. For they were together as a pair, they understood each other and each other's method of play. Best of all, no shadow of a possible separation hung over them because both felt that with the chance to prove what they could do, they'd never be split again. Chances came often, and they took advantage of them.

There was the series against the Cubs, in the first game of which Mallard, ever a dangerous pitcher, was facing the Dodgers. Going into the eighth, Brooklyn had worked into a three to nothing lead, but the eighth was almost always a dangerous inning for an old-timer like Rats Doyle, in the box for the Dodgers. Accordingly as the inning started Crane gave the warm-up signal, and two pitchers rose in the bullpen and began firing to their catchers. Just as well, for a base on balls was followed by a sacrifice and a two-bagger that sent Roy Tucker scurrying to the fence. One run over and a man on second. Big Elmer McCaffrey lumbered across the field and Rats, throwing his glove in disgust to the ground, walked off to the showers.

Elmer was ordered to pass the next man, a good hitter, and there were runners on first and second with only one out. The next batter hit a grounder past McCaffrey in the box, a slow roller which had to be picked up on the run with precious little time in which to do it. Spike was forced to "grab it by the handle" and let it go, for it was one of those plays in which half a step either way meant the decision.

Advancing for the ball, he knew it was impossible to make the long throw to first and, scooping it up, he tossed it underhand toward his brother who was racing in to second from his position on the grass. Bob came in a few steps ahead of the runner, caught the ball on the dead run just as he reached the bag and, without pausing, shot it to Harry Street on third. The whole thing was one movement done in an instant. The Cub runner from second had turned the corner at third and was several paces off the base before he saw what was coming. He dove for safety. Too late. A doubleplay and the side was out.

Now that Bob was on the team he felt completely sure of himself. He was the first man out for practice in the morning, the last man dressed in the afternoon, so tired he could hardly put his clothes on, so tired that after dinner he wanted only to lie down and sleep. For he was giving all the time, giving with strength and nervous energy, and his pep and chatter around second base were a tonic both the infield and the whole team badly needed.

The fans observed at once how the team snapped back. From fourth place they moved to third as the season drew to a close. The whole squad began making plays they hadn't been making for weeks. That combination around sec- ond was a shot in the arm to every man on the club. The team noticed it; so did the bleachers; so did the sportswriters who followed them from day to day.

"These Russell boys," wrote Jim Foster in the *Times,* "are as different as chalk and cheese. They're both baseball rookies making their first appearance in the big leagues; they're both good, and there the resemblance ends. Spike, the elder, is quiet and conscientious; Bob, the younger, is rowdy and raucous. Besides being Ginger Crane's solution to the infield problem that has been bothering the little manager all season, both boys have the ability to make the tough ones look easy. They're the cuffs on the trousers to the rooters, and this kid Bob is poison to left-handed lowball hitters. These Dodger freshmen may turn out to be one of the finest keystone combinations in baseball."

8

Winter. Snow was falling that evening in mid-February when Spike got back after work to their room in Mrs. Hampton's boarding-house on McGavock Street to find Bob triumphantly waving a telegram.

"It's from him, from Jack MacManus! Says he's passing through town next week and wants to see us about the contract. Gee, Spike, I sure hope we can fix things up. It looks like you were right after all."

As the business manager of the pair, Spike had confidence in his dealings with the Dodger management that was not entirely shared by his brother. Before leaving Brooklyn last fall he had consulted Fat Stuff at some length as to what kind of a contract they should ask for the next season. The veteran's opinion was that the Dodgers' Keystone Kids deserved a substantial raise.

"What'd you boys knock down this year?"

"I was paid on a basis of three thousand five, and Bobby three straight," answered Spike, talking baseball figures to the old pitcher.

He thought a while. "Well, let's see. The team finished up in third place, and you boys both had more than a little to do with our standing. Judging by your play out there, I'd say you were worth considerable more next year. Guess you oughta double it, say fifteen. Split it anyway you like—or they do."

But the contracts that arrived unsigned in Nashville shortly after Christmas called for a five thousand dollar salary to Spike and four to Bob. Somewhat to Bob's distress, Spike insisted on returning them immediately, unsigned, with a polite letter. "There's some guys think it's fine to holler and curse the management, but I think we'd be smart to leave Ginger an out."

"Yeah, an' suppose they don't take the out. Suppose they don't come back at us."

"They will," Spike assured him. "They got to.

75

They don't expect you to sign the first contract; they just send it out in hopes, that's all."

He was correct. The contract was returned with a raise of a thousand dollars apiece, making eleven thousand in all. Once again Bob was worried. Not Spike.

"No, sir, we're in a strong position. They need us bad out there round second base, and they know it. Besides, we got a leverage on 'em; we can make a living outside of baseball and they realize it. You got a good electrical job, haven't you? O.K., and I can always work in the L. and N. freight house. We got something to bargain with, boy."

"But we don't want to do that; we don't want to work here in Nashville. We wanna play baseball."

"Sure we do. But we can if we hafta, see? Point is, they need us bad. Now just sit tight and wait and see."

The contract went back unsigned.

Three days later a telephone call came for Spike in the Louisville and Nashville freight house where he was working. It caught him when the boss and three helpers were able to listen with interest. They only heard Spike's answers but they got enough to understand the meaning of the conversation.

"Spike?" It was the taut, aggressive voice of Ginger Crane. "Spike, let's get down to brass tacks. How much do you boys want anyhow?"

"We want fifteen, Ginger, split any way you folks like up there."

"Wow! Boy, have you got a nerve! For a couple of rookies in the big leagues, you got your gall. When I broke in with the Senators in '35 . . ."

Spike knew that record. "Yeah? This boy Wakefield, the kid who signed with the Tigers, got forty-two five," he answered in baseball terminology, hoping the railway men around wouldn't get it.

"What say? I don't believe it. Those are newspaper figures. At any rate, you boys haven't proved a thing so far, not a thing . . ."

"Nothing except we made eighteen double-plays that last month."

"What's that mean? Now that Ed Davis's arm is mended, I probably shan't use your brother except as a utility infielder next season."

"Well, Ginger, that's what we feel we're worth—fifteen."

"O.K., Spike, you know your own business best. I'd be mighty sorry to see you go, but that's how things are. So long, and good luck to you both."

He hung up. The click of the telephone had an impressively decisive tone that was unpleasant to hear, and Spike turned back to the open-mouthed freight-hands feeling unusually foolish.

Three or four days later a telegram arrived informing them that the raises were revoked. This really bothered both boys. What did that mean? They decided that it meant that if they signed now they'd have to do so at the figures of their original contracts—five and four thousand respectively. With difficulty Spike withstood his brother's pleas to write for a contract and sign immediately. A week later he was glad he hadn't weakened. A letter came from the manager saying he had no authority to treat further with them, and that from now on negotiations were in the hands of Jack MacManus, the fiery-tempered owner of the Dodgers. The letter didn't describe him that way, however.

No word came from that worthy, either, for almost ten days, and then late in January, when they were both worried and having trouble getting to sleep at night, a telephone call caught them one evening at the boarding-house. Spike took the call, wondering just which MacManus he would find at the other end. There was MacManus genial and charming; MacManus aroused and crazy mad; MacManus eager and attentive; MacManus keen and sober; Mac-Manus keen and not so sober. He was truly a man of moods. He could be agreeable and friendly, as he had been when they'd first come up, and in two minutes he could be as cold as ice.

To Spike's relief, MacManus was in his genial mood. "I really oughtn't to do this, but I'm fond of you boys and, confidentially, I'm going to break one of our club rules. Those raises are back in your contracts."

Spike was pleased by this generosity but somehow managed to keep his self-control.

"Yessir. Thank you very much indeed, sir."

"Then it's settled?"

"Nosir."

"What d'you mean, no?"

"Insufficient moolah, Mr. MacManus. We got good jobs down here; we can live on what we earn. And I feel we're worth fifteen to the club, sir."

Would he get mad? Would he rant and roar?

Would he bellow and call names over the phone? Not at all.

"O.K., Spike," he replied in his suavest tone. "I'm terribly sorry. I always liked you two boys, fine type of fellows, kind of lads we like to have on the club. But this is your last chance. Come now, don't you want to take a few days to think things over?"

"We have, sir."

"All right, all right. That's everything I've got to say then." Once again the telephone clicked decisively.

More unpleasant was the arrival of a letter which followed immediately. It was a nice letter, too nice in fact. The genial and charming MacManus wrote that they would both be missed next summer on the team. But after all business was business, so he wished them good luck in their new venture.

"What new venture?" snorted Bob. "Now then, see what you've done! You sure pulled a boner this time. He's through with us; he's washed us up. Because why? Just on account you're so doggoned stubborn. You held out for a few thousand and where are we? We're out, that's where we are!"

Spike, too, was upset this time. He simply

wouldn't have believed it, and somehow even yet it didn't make sense. He knew enough baseball to realize that Ed Davis with his arm at its best was not as good a man as Bob around second, not from any angle. And they needed a fast pair at that keystone sack if they hoped to overhaul the Pirates or the Cards, who were also improved. The fans liked them, too, the fans were for them, the fans and the writers as well.

"Shucks, I b'lieve he's stalling. If he isn't, he isn't. We must sit tight, Bob. We aren't through, not by any means. Nine thousand is just fishcakes; so is eleven. Maybe Grouchy will take us on. I hear they're talking of Grouchy as manager for the Cards next season."

But both boys spent some bad nights for a week until suddenly a wire arrived from Buffalo, New York. "HAVE A CHANCE TO BUY YOUR CONTRACTS STOP WOULD YOU PLAY WITH US PLEASE REPLY BY WESTERN UNION COLLECT IMMEDIATELY REGARDS STEVE O'HARE MANAGER."

Bob agreed at once to Spike's reply. "IF WE WOULDNT PLAY WITH THE DODGERS WE CERTAINLY WOULDNT PLAY WITH BUFFALO SPIKE AND BOB RUSSELL."

Then followed another week of uncertainty and suspense until the telegram came from

MacManus, who was on his way South, saying that he would stop off en route. Now Bob began to feel that possibly Spike's tactics had been correct. But he was extremely nervous as they both went upstairs in the elevator of the Andrew Jackson that evening to the boss's room, Spike in his working overalls, Bob in the clothes he wore on his electrical job. This was the older brother's idea. He wanted the owner of the club to see they weren't fooling.

That evening it was the genial MacManus, agreeable, affable, putting them at their ease, remembering they didn't smoke, pouring out double cokes for them; in short, Mac at his most charming. Two contracts were spread out on a table in one corner of the room. Evidently this time he meant business.

He lighted a cigarette. "Now, boys, I'm going to be frank with you; I'm going to put my cards on the table and take you both behind the scenes so you'll understand why we cannot under any consideration pay you more than eleven thousand dollars. Let me explain. These figures I'm telling you are seen by no one except the owner and stockholders of the club. They concern things you maybe never thought about, you probably didn't even know.

"Boys, we get, as the visiting team, twenty-three cents for every customer when we're away from home. We pay out twenty-three cents for every customer to all visiting clubs at Ebbets Field. Those are National League rules. We have nothing to say about them. Now where does all the money we take in go? Last year we played to a million here at home and over a million on the road. Well, we spent $180,000 on salaries, yours and Fat Stuff's and Razzle's and the Slugger's and the rest. That doesn't count what we pay our manager, the Doc, the rubbers, the clubhouse boy, and so forth and so on. Then we spent $19,856 for railroad fares. You travel well, don't you, boys? Yep, and that costs us money. Your uniforms were worth exactly $4,626. We spent $8,111 for baseballs. Your bats alone cost the club $632."

He spoke the words slowly, rolling over the figures on his tongue.

"I made out a check the other day to the Brooklyn Laundry for $6,789 for cleaning your uniforms, your underwear, and the towels. Away from home your hotel bills amounted to $17,146."

He was certainly a wonderful man. Figures rippled from his lips as he continued.

"And so on. You like a nice, good bounding ball, don't you, Spike, when you get set out there at short? You, too, Bob? So do the other boys. O.K. Our sprinkler system to keep the grass fresh and the turf solid so you'll get good bounds meant $10,000 last summer. Know what the lights cost? About $1,000 a month. I spent two-fifty grand repairing the stands and having the posts sunk in concrete last year. Then there's the amortization, depreciation, ushers' wages, groundkeepers, loss due to rain . . ."

Bob was dazed by this Niagara of figures. So, too, was Spike. But not completely. He interrupted the owner. "Yessir, yessir, I can see you have to spend a lot of money."

He suddenly produced a bill from his pocket and extended it toward the business man.

"Mr. MacManus, sir, here's a five spot if it'll help you any."

MacManus started in his chair. He would either lose his temper or laugh heartily at himself. There was a moment of tension in the room, broken by his explosion of merriment.

He roared with laughter. "Spike, you're a card! Well now, boys, what do you say? This'll give you an inside, a really inside picture of the situation. You both started well for us but, of course, we have to recognize that you slumped a bit there toward the end."

"Yessir. And we made forty-eight doubleplays while we were up with the club, Mr. MacManus. That's . . . that's . . ."

By the expression on his face, Spike saw the owner had been talking with Ginger Crane.

"Doubleplays! Doubleplays! Do doubleplays get a man on first? Hits win ballgames. Now, boys, I'm sure we understand each other. I've got just so much money, and even if you made a doubleplay in every chance you handled I couldn't pay you five cents more. I've put back those ups in your contract; that means eleven between the two of you. But I want to be generous, I want to do the right thing by you. I appreciate you did a good job jumping in there the way you both did the end of the season. So suppose we say twelve. That gives you six apiece. Six for both of you, how's that, hey?"

He looked at them closely, seeing Bob's tense, eager expression. What the older boy was thinking and how he would respond to this offer Jack MacManus had no idea nor could his brother, searching that face for a hint, guess either.

"Yes, sir. Yes, Mr. MacManus," said Spike at last. "I'd like to be able to sign up but it just wouldn't be fair to you, sir. We wouldn't be able to do our best for you."

Now MacManus was annoyed. He had made concessions, too many concessions. They'd sign now, by ginger, or else . . .

"Boys, this is your last chance. I really mean business." He looked it, too. His grimness frightened Bob, who turned to his brother.

"Spike, I think we oughta sign for twelve, don't you?"

Then Jack MacManus, a rare judge of human nature, made one of his rare mistakes.

"O.K. If he won't sign, how 'bout you putting your John Hancock on that contract, Bob? I promise you won't be sorry."

No one spoke. The silence lasted and lasted.

"You mean . . . I should leave Spike, Mr. MacManus?" What was the man saying? Leave Spike and go back up there alone? Not a chance!

MacManus, shrewd, intelligent, realized instantly he had made a bad mistake. But before he could correct himself the boy replied.

"Thank you very much indeed, sir, but I reckon I better stick with my brother."

"What? Why, you young fatheads! You fresh young bushers . . . throwing away your last chance . . . you two chowderheads! This *is* your last chance . . . don't you appreciate . . ."

Now he was angry. MacManus liked to jockey with other people, but he enjoyed winning these battles and he usually did win. When losing he didn't enjoy himself at all. And he was losing, he knew he was losing, although the two scared boys did not. For almost the first time in the long weeks of indecision, Spike was thoroughly frightened as the Dodger owner, red in the face, rose from his chair, strode across the room, took the two contracts off the table and hurled them over.

"Take 'em, take 'em, you young bushers, you fresh young rookies . . . you . . ."

They reached over and each picked up a contract from the floor. Both contracts were made out in typewritten figures for the same sum—seven thousand five hundred dollars!

9

The Florida sun beat down on the small ballpark so reminiscent of those the Russell boys had known in their minor league days; on the veterans and the rookies, on Slugger Case and Fat Stuff and Elmer McCaffrey, who knew all the answers and worked out slowly and deliberately; on Ginger Crane, the manager, no longer on the active list for the first time in his fourteen seasons in the majors; and on the Russell boys cavorting like two ponies in the dust behind second base. Standing in the rear of the batting cage, Ginger surveyed his squad and listened to Bob Russell, the chatterbox of the team, in action.

"Uhuh, he does more talking than all the rest of the team put together. Shoot, we needed some chin music out there; it helped toward the end of last season. We'd never have finished third without those kids in there."

"Ginger, do you expect to play those boys together, or will you break 'em up and shove Ed Davis in?" asked one of the sportswriters.

"I can't tell, can't tell a thing. Too early yet. Depends on how the kid shapes up, how Ed's arm holds out, on a lot of different things. Listen to him out there now."

From the dust of the infield came the harsh, brazen chatter of the little second baseman. "Boy, you gotta get your hands round that thing," he yelled to a rookie outfielder. "You have to get your hands round it; there aren't any handles on the ball."

Spring training was a grind, yet Spike and Bob enjoyed it. For one thing, much of it was new to them. They liked being with a big league club, liked living in a comfortable and luxurious hotel; they liked the players, no longer strange faces but friends; most of all they liked this chance to show what they really could do without the pressure of the pennant race to tighten them up. The only thing they really disliked was the badgering of the newspapermen who pestered them continually.

Nothing bothered Spike and Bob in all baseball as much as this interviewing. Once during the second week of spring training, a reporter was trying hard to get a story from them.

"Just what do you boys find is the main difference between the majors and the minors?"

They looked quickly at each other. As usual, Spike spoke for the pair. "The pitchers, I'd say. A man faces a good pitcher every day in the week up here. Down at Nashville we used to have a lamb every now and then to fatten up the old batting average. When you come up to the majors you don't notice much difference at first except that the pitchers are all tough."

"Isn't the fielding better?"

"Sure is. Everything's faster; there's . . . oh . . . there's a lot of little things; more polish; the hitters don't go after the bad balls so much."

Yet deep in their hearts both boys felt there was one difference they wouldn't discuss with any writer. That was the difference they most noticed—the difference in managers.

Grouchy Devine was a laconic, deeply religious Irishman who went to Mass each morning, a man of great sensitivity and a feeling of affection for every one of his twenty-five players. To him every man was an individual problem to be solved. He was quiet, kept to himself off the grounds. In their stay on the Vols they had learned enormously from him, but they had never seen him criticize a player in public nor ever dispute an umpire's decision. In fact, his reputation for grouchiness came mostly from the fact that he stayed away from reporters asking for interviews about the team. Whenever one of the sportswriters asked him early in the season, "Well, Grouchy, how does the team look?" he would wave his hand in the direction of his perspiring athletes and reply, "There they are. Take a look for yourself."

This did not endear him to the press. But the two brothers had often heard him growl in the dressing room, after evading a reporter in search of a story, "When you don't say anything, you don't never have to eat your own words." Spike and Bob remembered this line in their own dealings with the sportswriters covering the Dodgers in spring training, and talked as little as possible to the gentlemen of the press.

Ginger Crane was exactly Grouchy's opposite. He was loud, loquacious, liked to talk and be with talkative people who were good listeners, as well. He was quick, nervous, excitable, and in action could always be depended on to do the unexpected. His relations with the press astonished the two Russells. Where Grouchy avoided newspapermen at all times, Ginger hobnobbed with them, ate with them occasionally, even went on fishing trips with them. He was never reluctant to discuss the chances of his team or any team in the league. He was bold, belligerent on the field, and it seemed to the boys he was on the field a good part of every game. He delighted in battles with the umpires or with opposing players, and he thought no more of being sent to the clubhouse than of ordering his dinner at night.

Ginger ran his team on hunches, shifting his fielders about like chessmen, and throwing in pitcher after pitcher until some games resembled the dying moments of a football battle with substitutes pouring in to get their letters. On hunches he had won one pennant, and notwithstanding his setback of the previous summer he was confident he could win again. Spike and Bob had imagined that his nervousness of the year before was due entirely to the strain of the pennant race. Not at all. Ginger was just as tense in a practice game between the regulars and the yannigans in that little bandbox under the Florida sun.

●

The two Russells were dressing for the second exhibition game against the Giants at Miami, listening to the merry chatter of the locker room as the team prepared for the afternoon's workout.

"What's this-here-now Harris—fella used to play third for the Yankees—what's he doing now?" asked a voice.

"I understand he's coaching at Yale."

"Coaching baseball at Yale!" Ginger's contemptuous tone dominated the room. "Shoot! He can do that mornings over the telephone."

There was a burst of genuine laughter. Ginger was one manager at whose jokes a guy could really laugh. Spike bit at the top of his sweatshirt as he put it under his supporter, holding it in his teeth by one end to be sure to give himself freedom under the arms. He liked to be nice and loose in his movements and hated clothes that hampered him in any way. While he picked up his sliding pads, Bob was climbing into a pair of basketball pants. This was about the only thing on which the two brothers ever disagreed—the merits of these garments for sliding into bases. Spike heard Cassidy's voice, strong, acidulous.

". . . Well, seems some 12-year-old kid came up to the Giant manager last week and asked for a try-out. He was nice to the kid, told him to wait a few years and come back again later. Today the same boy shows up and asks for a try-out once more. 'Why, looka here,' says the manager, 'I thought I told you last week to come back here when you was a few years older.' 'Well, Mister,' says this kid, 'I watched your Giants take that nine to nothing licking against the Dodgers yesterday, and that aged me ten years.'"

Guffaws broke out over the room. The team was certainly feeling good.

Spike sat down on the bench before his locker and drew on his inner socks. They came below his knees and he fastened them with rubber garters. As he leaned over, he observed Razzle drawing on two pairs, one over the other. Raz had thin legs for a big man and was notoriously vain. It was little things such as these that amazed the boys about these big leaguers; Razzle's vanity, Swanson's tightness with money, Jake Kennedy's superstitions. They were a strange lot with queer contradictions in their make-up.

Meanwhile Razzle's voice dominated the room.

"A raise? Mebbe I did get me a raise. Why shouldn't I get a raise?" He was talking with the *New York Times* reporter who stood with his hands in his pockets watching Raz climb into his clothes. "Won twenty games last year, didn't I, and got the Most Valuable Player Award?"

The reporter winked at Bob who was in the act of hauling his outer shirt on and fastening it up. "I thought Mac Ennis of the Cards got the Most Valuable Player Award, Razzle."

"They give it to him. They give it to him; but I should have been give it. I really won it," said Razzle with his customary fine disdain for the niceties of the English language. "When that-there committee met, they musta gone into a transom."

"Raz, your English is really something," remarked Fat Stuff.

"Yeah, and my Spanish is something, too. Say, Fat Stuff, a guy I know who lived in Havana told me the Spanish have no word for shortstop. Whadd'ya think of that?"

"I wouldn't worry if I were you, Razzle," said the old pitcher. "Neither have the Phillies."

More laughter. Spike pulled on his pants and

buckled his elastic belt. Throwing off his shower shoes which he wore until almost the last minute, he sat down and put on his uniform socks of wool, and then leaned over for his shoes. Those shoes were expensive, made of kangaroo skin, and ballplayers pay for their own shoes. Both he and his brother were always ripping and tearing them in the scrimmages around second base, and to his dismay he had figured out that morning they would probably spend $150 and wear out five or six pairs of shoes apiece during the season.

Down the line Razzle was still talking. Finally he finished dressing, picked up his glove, and stalked out.

"There goes the All-American adenoid," said Karl Case, scorn in his voice. A titter ran over the room. Spike looked down at Bob pulling on his inner socks and Bob looked up at Spike. Both were thinking the same thing and understood each other without talking. What a difference from Grouchy and the Volunteers! There was a real team. Those boys had no groups or factions. For a second both felt homesick for that familiar atmosphere. True, there was never a dull moment, never a day when some trick wasn't pulled or someone given a hotfoot, never a dull moment on the Dodgers. And yet . . .

Yet there were times when both longed for the quieter, smoother methods of old Grouchy, unspectacular, unpretentious, always the same if you did your job and gave your best on the field. A manager sets the tone for the club, and Ginger's team was almost as argumentative and disputatious among themselves as with other teams on the field and with the umpires.

"Spike," said Ginger, taking him by the arm while they were having batting practice before the game, "just run out there and tell Case I want to see him a minute, will ya?"

Spike trotted out to left where the swarthy outfielder was catching flies. "Hey, Karl, Ginger wants to see you."

Karl paused, his hands on his hips. "What's the matter with his eyesight? Can't he see me from there?" And to Spike's amazement he continued chasing flies.

Old Fat Stuff was standing alone on the coaching line as Spike walked back, wondering what he should do. He told the veteran pitcher. "That guy Case, he's a card," said Spike, explaining what had happened.

The pitcher pulled off his cap and wiped his

brow with the sleeve of his sweatshirt. Then he replaced the cap on his head. "Don't he get along with Ginger?" asked Spike. "I always thought they were old pals."

"They were. They used to be. But not now. There's too darned many factions on this club."

The umpires appeared and the two players walked back to the bench. Spike was by no means new to baseball, and he realized that with thirty men living together everyone couldn't feel alike, that pitchers thought differently about things from anyone else, that cliques and relationships were bound to develop. Even so, he wondered, how could a ballclub in this mental condition hope to win a pennant even with high-powered hitters in the line-up?

That afternoon trouble broke out openly. The game was close and old Raz was in command all the way. In the eighth with a two-run lead, he was hit on the side of the head between innings by a ball thrown accidentally by Harry Street. The ball bounced high in the air and Raz stood ruefully rubbing his forehead, while Harry raced over solicitously, and soon the entire infield surrounded him. Only Case, in left field, maintained an attitude of neutrality about the whole affair by turning his back and calmly sitting down on the grass.

Finally Raz resumed play. A lump rose on the side of his forehead. In the eighth the Giants got a run when Harry fielded a bunt too slowly. In the last of the ninth with Brooklyn ahead 2-1, Giants were on first and second with two out. The center fielder came to bat. Spike, nervous, turned and saw Karl Case retiring deep in the field. A blooper to short left would cause trouble, and he waved the veteran in but Case paid no attention. Razzle's first pitch was hit to left. Ordinarily it would have been an easy out, one of those hits that don't mean a thing. But Karl, playing deep to protect himself, found it hard to handle. He came thundering in and made a desperate stab for the ball. It burned through his fingers to the fence while both runners scored and the two teams dashed for the showers.

Disconsolately the squad trooped inside. Not knowing Karl was close behind him, Raz kept grumbling half to himself. ". . . Any outfielder oughta be able to catch a ball coming in. . . ."

Whereat Karl, to no one in particular, paid his respects to pitchers, remarking that "If they'd get the ball over the plate once in a while, we might win games." On this note the team poured into the dressing room. Spike observed that the lump on Razzle's forehead was as big as an egg. The unlucky pitcher slumped down on the bench while Doc Masters applied hot towels soaked in witch hazel to reduce the swelling, and Raz kept muttering something over and over which sounded like "Clumsy butterfingers." Everyone knew Karl had played too far back in order to protect himself.

However, the Slugger was far from upset by his error. He kept talking in the showers in loud tones for the benefit of his friends and anyone who happened to be listening, amid loud guffaws. "Yeah, they rushed the ball to the Miami General Hospital, and the docs operated. That's right, they had to take two stitches in the darn thing."

His voice could be heard pretty much all over the lockers, despite the noise and roar of the showerbaths. When he emerged, Raz kept muttering to himself as Case went past to his locker, a bath towel around his waist.

Just beyond Razzle he stopped, turned, and came back. "What's that? What was that you said just now? What was that you called me, Raz?"

Poor Razzle's head was throbbing and he was in misery.

"I said you was a clumsy, butterfingered clown," he remarked, rising to go to the showers.

As he did so, Case reddened and lunged. He struck Raz on the undamaged part of his face and staggered him. But Raz came right back, both fists thrashing the air, whacking and pounding at Case's body. They grappled. Benches shot across the room; clothes, shoes, the whole dressing room went round and round in a cyclone of noise as the two men wrestled, tripped, tumbled, and sprawled to the floor. While Ginger, the Doc, the coaches, and old Chiselbeak, the locker room attendant, jumped to pull them apart.

Sometimes a fight in which both men shake hands afterwards clears the atmosphere. But Spike and Bob knew there would be no hand-shaking after this one. They sat there transfixed to the bench, eyes popping. Seldom had they seen this kind of a row before. Soberly they dressed and soberly returned to the hotel, saying little, both thinking the same thing. Gosh, how on earth can we hope to catch the Pirates when we scrap like that among ourselves?

They were more sober after reading the evening paper. Spike went to the hotel lobby where Swanson was standing as usual by the newsstand.

He glanced over Spike's shoulder. "Well, whadd'ya think of that! Say, what do you think . . ." He pointed to a column halfway down the front page.

It was a despatch from St. Petersburg where the Cards were in training. Their manager had left and Grouchy Devine, the veteran pilot of the Nashville Vols, had been appointed to take over. Spike read the headlines and read them again. He turned toward his brother.

"Hey, Bobby," he called, "just look at this!"

10

When a team picked to win the pennant starts the season badly, it's not hard to explain to the public. But when April turns into May and the same team is dragging anchor in third place, when May dies away and June draws near and they are solidly anchored in fourth, there's trouble ahead. The wisecracks start appearing in the newspapers, sports editors assign cub reporters to follow the team or drop out altogether on the club's next western trip. When this happened to the Dodgers, most of the trouble seemed to fall upon the broad shoulders of that diplomat and business man combined, Bill Hanson, the club secretary.

He had plenty to do. For as the days became longer and warmer, nerves became tauter. Inside the club, cliques developed. Some players refused to speak to others, and the two Russell boys had to be more careful than ever what they said casually to men with whom they traveled or to whom they talked in the dugout. You could never tell with the club in such a situation whose feelings you might hurt, or when you might unknowingly step into a nasty situation. Hanson was busy all day and much of the night smoothing out quarrels, arranging things after Ginger had talked indiscreetly to some sportswriter, settling as best he could the daily bickerings. And meanwhile the Dodgers continued to slide slowly down in the league standing.

Things got so bad that MacManus hired and sent on from New York an Austrian psychiatrist to travel with the team and straighten them out. He was introduced all round as the team physician, this causing no small amount of disgust to Doc, the trainer, who felt he knew as much as anyone about the conditioning of athletes. The psychiatrist's first rule, that everyone should be down for breakfast at nine-thirty in the morning, did nothing to make the stranger popular with the team. It's a long while from nine-thirty to game time, and longer still when play is at night. Ballplayers don't enjoy sitting around a hotel lobby doing nothing all day any more than other people do.

Game after game was dropped and Ginger Crane grew tense. His tenseness, plainly observable by everybody, communicated itself to the entire squad. The moment a pitcher showed signs of faltering he was taken out. The result was a constant procession of men from the bullpen in deep right field to the box and soon afterward to the showers. It made funny reading the next morning in the newspapers to see three, four, or five pitchers in the Dodgers' box scores. Often a hurler would go in, throw four or five balls, and be replaced. Old Fat Stuff was in the bullpen so much of the time that, as Raz remarked, he got his mail there.

Whereas Grouchy had seldom shifted his fielders, playing them mostly straightaway, Ginger shifted them for every batter, placing them now toward right, now toward left, always trying to outguess the hitters. Sometimes he did. Almost every day the batting order was shaken up. One day you were in the clean-up position, the next in the sixth spot. He played Whitehouse, a substitute, at third for several games when Street fell into a batting slump, and only let Swanson go to bat against right-handed pitching because he hit left-handed. Against left-handers he threw in young Paul Roth, a right-handed batter. When Karl Case went into a batting slump, Ginger put in Clyde Baldwin, a rookie outfielder, to rest the veteran for a week, he said.

The result was to mix everyone up completely. Swanson complained that he hardly got his eye in before he was taken out of the game, and that when he got back it took him several days to get his eye again. No wonder he was batting .218! Red Allen became home-run conscious, and started swinging off his heels at the plate. With the sluggers striking out and hitting pop flies, the Russell boys, who had never been tremendous power-houses at the plate, tried to assume responsibility for the hitting of the team. Naturally their batting fell off. Bones Hathaway, a promising young pitcher who had won five games, had the nail torn off the little finger of his pitching hand by a line drive. It seemed bad luck could go no further. The Russells had never played on such a team. Daily they could watch the worsening of the club's morale.

That afternoon they managed to lose another

close game to the Reds. After getting three runs in the second, the Dodgers were caught in the fourth, and when Swanson missed a hard liner in deep right center, they were passed in the eighth. To the surprise of the Russells, accustomed to Grouchy's quieter and more subtle methods of handling players, Ginger assailed the fielder as soon as he returned to the bench, before everybody.

"Swanny, if you can't run any more, if you feel like you can't play right field the way it should be played, I'll hire someone who can."

The big fielder turned on him. "You waved me over toward the line, didn't you? That man's not a pull hitter. You oughta know that. If you think you can play right better than me, why don't you?"

Ginger lost his temper. His face was close to Swanson's. His jaw stuck out as it did when he went for an umpire on the field. "I would if I was a little younger." Then he collected himself and started out to the coaching line. Too late, for the whole team had heard the exchange and the bench was subdued during the rest of the game.

Silently they trooped into the dressing room after the defeat. On the notice board was a sign.

BROOKLYN BASEBALL CLUB. NEXT CITY, PITTS-

BURGH. TRAIN LEAVES UNION STATION AT 9:50 C.D.S. TIME. ARRIVES PITTSBURGH, 9:30 A.M. E.D.S. TIME. BAGGAGE READY AT 8:30 TONIGHT.

They sat around quietly, dressing slowly. For once even Razzle was depressed and silent.

"Man," said Bob under his breath, "we can't seem to win nohow. Wonder why we can't win?"

Someone next to him heard the remark. "Maybe the Quiz Kids could answer that one."

But there was little talking. They showered and got dressed, all except Spike who sat slumped on his bench, wondering what had happened to the team, what had happened to his own batting eye. He watched the little groups of players gathering around the room. When a ballclub breaks up into groups, Grouchy used to say, watch out.

Spike glanced up at his brother standing before him all dressed.

"No, I'm not ready. Don't wait for me, Bobby."

"Aw, c'mon, Spike. Let's us take in a movie tonight before the train leaves."

"Naw. I'm gonna lie down a while after dinner. I'll get me an early dinner and rest, I guess. I don't sleep so good on those Pullmans."

"Man, it'll do you good."

"No, I'll just rest a while. I'm tired. Say . . .

you know what? I b'lieve I was swinging too hard today. I thought I was swinging the same as when I got those three baggers last week; guess not though. Mebbe I was striding too soon or something. Oh, I guess it was just one of those days. Well, you run along. I'm gonna try to rest a while. See you later, Bobby."

Actually Spike never saw his brother until just before game time at Forbes Field, Pittsburgh, the next afternoon. Because Bob committed the unpardonable sin of losing track of the time and missed the train by forty minutes. He finally entered the Dodger dressing room just as the manager was finishing his usual pre-game harangue of the team.

"Here he is! You thought you'd come back, thought you'd show up after all, hey? It's a wonder you bothered," remarked the manager as he saw Bob in the doorway.

Spike knew the boy was due for a lacing in public and feared the effect it might have on his hot-tempered brother. Luckily, Bob was ashamed and chagrined.

Ginger continued before them all. "Well, Mister, you missed the train, didn't you? You stupid bonehead, didn't you see the notice posted in the locker room yesterday? You did?

How come you missed the train then? You know the rules of this club. Well, you were given a booklet same as everyone else; like all the rest you didn't bother to read it. That's too bad, because this will cost you exactly fifty soap bubbles. Now hustle into that monkey suit of yours, and let's see you do something out there for a change. Say! You got the ticket, didn't you?" He added this last as the team started for the diamond.

"What ticket?" The team paused.

Ginger instantly became red in the face. He was tired and he was worried; he was cross and needed little to set him off. This was the final straw. "The ticket Hanson left with the station-master. He left your ticket on the 11:30 with the stationmaster. D'you mean to tell me you didn't have brains enough to ask for it?"

For once Bob was confused. "Why . . . no . . . I didn't know . . . I didn't think . . . ."

"Didn't think! Didn't think! Didn't think!" roared Ginger. "O.K. That'll cost you fifty bucks more, what do you think of that? Will that make you think, will it? And you can have the privilege of paying for your own ticket to Pittsburgh, too. Now maybe the next time you will think. That is, if you stay on this club and there is any next time, and I ain't saying you're staying, either. We can trade men up to June 15th, you fellows know. You also know we're carrying twenty-eight men now and we have to cut down to twenty-five in the next ten days-two weeks. C'mon now, don't stand there gawping. Get out and play baseball, that's what you're paid for. My gosh, the only thing you guys can do is play baseball and you're too damn lazy to do that."

The day had started badly. "Aw, the big lug, picking on your kid brother that way," remarked Case to Spike, as they clattered down the concrete runway to the field. Inside Spike was angry, but he couldn't say much. After all, Bob had missed the train. "Oh, he had to do it; he's upset, he doesn't mean anything by it."

"Has to do nothing! That's not a rule of this club."

"It isn't?"

"Of course not. He wouldn't dare pull that one on me or any of us who knew our way round. He does it to your kid brother because he's a rookie. The rules say the manager shall fine a player *if* he misses a train and doesn't get to the field in time to start the game. He got here, got here an hour and a half before game time. Nuts to that, picking on a freshman like your brother, the first time he slipped, too. Ginger only did it for effect, anyway."

"For effect?" He was puzzled.

"Why, sure! If we'd been leading the league, do you think he'd have done that? He would not. We're on the skids, see, and he's on the skids, too, and he knows it. MacManus is plenty sore; he's hammering away at Crane every day by telegraph and telephone from Brooklyn, asking him how come, and what's the matter with the team. See now, when this comes out, when MacManus reads about this in the sports pages back home, it sort of excuses Ginger for the team's poor showing; makes it look as if the boys aren't cooperating. Heck, we haven't had a real manager on this club since old Dave Leonard left. As for that Crane, I played with him in Chicago. He's mean, he's really mean. Why, the man's so mean he washes his own socks."

11

"Read that, Spike," said his brother, passing over the sports pages of the newspaper. They were on their way out to the field in a street car. In Pittsburgh most of the players went from the William Penn to the field in a taxi, but the Russell boys frequently walked. When they didn't, they rode in the street cars. What's the use of spending fifty cents, they figured, when you have all the time on earth and can get there for a dime.

The article was in the *Post-Gazette*, an interview with Ginger Crane. It was typical of Ginger. Grouchy, now leading the league with his hard-hitting Cardinals, was as reticent and difficult to interview as he had been in the minors. But Ginger talked on every occasion, although he was no longer a pennant contender. Whether his team was in first place or last, he always had something to say to the sportswriters.

"Yes, I have a team of .400 hitters—switch hitters, .200 from each side. And a one-man pitching staff, too. What's that mean? I'll explain. It's easy. We're carrying eight pitchers on the payroll. O.K. Bones Hathaway lost the fingernail on his pitching hand last week; that makes seven. Rats Doyle is so old he aches all over; that makes six. Fat Stuff Foster has a bad cold. O.K., that makes five. Jake Kennedy has trouble putting it across in the pinches; that makes four. McCaffrey has a sore arm; that makes . . . how many . . . three. Speed Boy Davis hasn't rounded into form yet this year; he's always a late starter for me; that makes two. Razzle Nugent thinks his bunion is troubling him; that leaves one. Roger Stinson—a one-man pitching staff. Get it?"

Spike handed back the newspaper without reading further. "That guy! He's a name manager, that's what he is, always getting his name in the paper, always popping off in public. He loves it."

"Yeah, he sure loves to talk out loud. I mean he thinks out loud; that's his trouble."

They descended from the trolley at the Schenley and walked down the short street to the ballpark. No crowd was gathering, no one assaulted them for autographs, no policemen were waiting for on-rushing crowds at the gate. When you're in the second division, when you're holding down fifth place, the fans manage to let you alone. Inside the clubhouse things looked even more dismal. The day was dark and chilly and the high-walled dressing room with its barren stone floor seemed more gloomy than ever. Two antique gas heaters, which ought to have been in a museum, were sputtering feebly, and the Doc was grumbling as he tried to work on McCaffrey's sore arm.

"Gee, I'd sure hate to play on this-here club, even if they are up there in second place," remarked Razzle, looking around.

"Yeah, I played two years on the Phils," said Red Allen. "They don't pay big salaries on the Phils but they have a decent dressing room. And they travel first class."

"Lemme tell you something," called Roger from the table. "Until you've been on the Browns you don't know from nothing. It's mebbe different now under Leonard, but when I was on the club the secretary walked through the diner and slapped a buck and a half down beside your plate. Makes a guy feel he's on a lousy club."

On a lousy club, that's it, everyone was thinking. We'll never go places under this guy Crane, never; it's a lousy ballclub.

Then at one side Spike noticed a new boy dressing; a tall boy, with jet black hair and a prominent nose. He had a good chest and a fine pair of shoulders. His face was sensitive and intelligent, and Spike observed he was watching and listening as the players pulled on their monkey suits without enthusiasm. Case walked past on the way to the Coca-Cola list pinned to the wall. He wrote his name down and took a bottle, pausing a minute to speak to Bill Hanson standing near by. His voice was low but Spike heard what he said.

"Bill! Look, I need some new sticks, and I got one here that suits me fine. I'd like to put in an order on Louisville for a dozen just like it."

The secretary seemed uninterested. He half turned away, and Spike could only catch part of his answer. It was enough. "Oh, don't you think you got enough, Karl, for the present?" Quite evidently he wasn't buying any more bats for

Case, which could only mean one thing. A deal was in the offing to trade the left fielder by June 15th. That was exactly what the fielder was trying to find out. He turned away abruptly and moved over to his locker, an untouched bottle of coke in his hand.

A few minutes later they clattered out of the dressing room. Anyone could notice the listless sound of their spikes on the concrete, clack . . . clack . . . clack . . . clack . . . clack.

"Well, looks like the old trade winds are blowing," said someone at Spike's elbow.

"What makes you think so, Swanny?"

The fielder raised his head knowingly. "We got ourselves another rookie today. If he stays, someone goes. We're carrying twenty-eight men without him."

"Yeah, that black-haired boy. I saw him. Who is he, d'you know?"

"Catcher by the name of Klein up from the Three I League to Rochester, and did better than all right last year, they say. He won't last here, though."

"No? Why not?"

"Jewish boy."

"Jewish boy?"

"That's right."

"Oh! Well, what of it?"

"He won't last, that's what of it. The bench jockeys will get him. You'll see. They'll ride that baby to death. Besides, these Jewish boys can't take it. Haven't any guts."

Spike started to answer but now they were on the field and he heard Case's heavy voice behind him.

"I'm maybe not hitting right now, but I'll betcha twenty-five bucks I pass Red Allen yet. You see if I don't."

That bird's a percentage Patsy, thought Spike, always thinking of his own batting averages. Now if he'd only think a little more of the team and a little less of his own batting averages, we might go places. That's the thing that hurts us.

They came onto the field to warm up, the sun now shining. It was the usual routine: the pepper game to start, the batting in the cage, the fielding practice, the fungo hitting to the fielders. Then he realized what Swanson meant by saying the newcomer wouldn't last on the Dodgers. The boy was standing alone at one side, going through strange contortions. First he would squat, then stand up, then wave both hands over his head, turn round twice, and suddenly dash off to one side or the other. Spike watched him closely for a moment.

Is he nuts? Is that his trouble? Why, no, he's practicing, practicing spinning, going for a foul fly. That isn't such a bad idea! Never heard of that, practicing spinning, but there's guys right on this club it would help. It would help Bobby and me. It would sure help some of those outfielders, too.

Then a stray ball rolled up behind the newcomer as he squatted down.

"Hey! Hey there, Buglenose," shouted someone. "Hey there, Buglenose, throw us that ball."

He knew who was meant. He stopped, straightened up, looked around, and saw the ball behind him. Would he respond to that name? He turned slowly, leaned over, picked up the ball and tossed it back. He had the snap throw catchers use returning balls to their pitcher.

The game started. It was a Monday crowd, barely three thousand spectators spattered over a park built to hold forty thousand. Great gaps showed in the lower stands, an empty yawning cavern in the upper ones, and vast reaches of blank seats in the bleachers. Like every ballplayer, Spike hated to perform to empty seats, and the game began on a dull note.

"Come on now, come on, wake up those bats," shouted Ginger desperately from the coaching lines. "C'mon, boys; c'mon, Case-boy, let's have a hit."

Case swung at the first ball. It looked like a hit and was indeed a hit, a hard driven shot between second and third. But the Pittsburgh shortstop, who had been playing well back on the grass, made a marvelous stop and pulled up to throw. All the while Case was straining, straining, straining, giving everything he had; he was almost there, he was caught, he was nipped!

No! The throw was a trifle wide. It yanked the first baseman off the bag long enough for Karl to flash past in safety. He slowed down, turned, and came back slowly to the base, panting. Suddenly the light on the scoreboard in center flashed, and he began jumping up and down in disgust. It was called an error for the shortstop, not a hit for him. Case, enraged, felt he had been cheated out of his hit, and standing on first he turned toward the press box high above the plate, where the official scorer sat. With the crowd watching, he motioned downward with his arms and palms. Then he put two fingers to his nose, pinching it.

Murmurs ran up and down the Dodger bench.

"Oh . . . that's bad . . . that's bad, Karl, that's really bad."

"Ask that guy what the score is and he'll tell you he got two hits for four times at bat!"

"Shucks, he's always thinking of his own hits."

"Keeps his batting average on his sleeve, that bird."

By the remarks and the tone in which they were made it was evident Case was far from popular on the club.

"Yeah, he had that one all figured out; he had his batting average all figured out before he hit first base. There's some guys on this club don't think of nothing but their batting average and the dinner menu." Case's appetite was famous.

The incident upset the manager also. When Red Allen struck out, with Case and Spike on base, he turned toward the bench, his hands flung out and an expression on his face that said, Well, what can you do with a team like this?

Red lumbered back to the dugout and sat down just in time to catch the gesture. The big, good-natured first baseman sank to his seat, disgusted. Like all of them, he hated to have the manager criticize him in public. He said nothing, but his folded arms and the scowl on his usually calm face told plainly how he felt.

With the score a tie at one to one in the fifth, and Swanson on second, Spike watched anxiously from the bench while his brother laid down a perfect bunt along the third base line.

If they get him, they'll have to step on it, thought Spike, as the boy's feet flashed toward first.

Actually, no play was made at all. Men were on first and third. Now the Pirate pitchers in the bullpen began bearing down, while Crane roared encouragement from third base. Suddenly the Pittsburgh catcher whipped a quick throw into third, and the baseman slapped the ball on Swanson as he slid back. It was a decision that could have gone either way.

Out? Out? In disgust Ginger threw the glove in his hand on the ground. Two out and a man on first, instead of men on first and third and one out. That's throwing it away. Crane stalked angrily in from the coaching lines, while Cassidy replaced him back of third. The peppery little manager was reaching the end of his rope. Hardly knowing what he was doing, he upset the bat rack with a kick of his foot, and then tossed a couple of white towels out onto the ground before the bench.

"Shoot! Shoot!" he muttered, when Swanny, just as angry, came sullenly in and sat down. "Shoot! Some of you birds see third so seldom you don't know how to act when you do get there."

Then Harry Street leaned into a fastball and sent it sizzling deep in far left field. "There you are! There you are!" shouted Crane, jumping up to the step. "There you are, what'd I tell you . . . there you are! We'd have had the ballgame if Swanson hadn't been asleep . . . WHAT . . . what! What's that . . ."

In one bound he was out of the dugout and rushing for the plate. Cassidy, the third base coach, and Draper, behind first, were there before him. The umpire had called the hit foul and was waving Harry back as he rounded second.

His jaw out, his fists clenched by his side, his upper lip curled back dangerously, the Dodger manager roared up to the plate umpire, already the center of more players than he liked. From the bench the rest of the team could hear that rasping voice, could see him pour the pent-up anger of weeks upon the unfortunate official. Across the way the Pirates jumped in to join the mob around the plate, everyone yelling at everyone else, shouting as they ran toward that seething mass of gesticulating ballplayers.

"It was . . . it was not . . . it was so . . . it was not, I say . . . I was right on the line, I tell ya . . . you big bum . . . O.K. . . . Wanna make something out of it . . . ?"

The umpire turned and walked majestically away. His back was to the plate and he moved slowly toward the stands, arms folded, his dignity unruffled. From the edge of the melee around the plate, the Russells could hear Ginger's invective as he chased along at the umpire's shoulder. His face was up close, his jaw out, every gesture threatening. Finally the official turned. Now he was angry.

"Crane . . . if you follow me two steps further, you're out of the game."

"Then I'm out, 'cause I'm gonna follow you." And he did.

The hand of the umpire went up, there was a shout from the sparse crowd, Crane was banished from the game. It was a sort of signal.

Suddenly a riot broke out about the plate, bats and fists were swinging, men went down, spikes glistened in the sunshine of late afternoon.

Gosh! I wish I was manager of this team, Spike thought. No, I don't either. I wish we were back on the Volunteers and out of this sort of thing.

12

So! Klein's a hitter, is he? He's a hitter, this rookie! O.K., the pitchers all said. Fine, we'll show him. We'll loosen him up; we'll let him have a look at big league stuff.

And they proceeded to throw at his head every time he came to bat. Bob noticed this immediately and mentioned it to Spike that night in their room in the Copley Plaza in Boston.

"Say, that boy Klein is sure taking it from the pitchers. They're throwing at his head. Seems like he's been on the ground most of every game he's played so far."

"Well, that's the correct treatment for a busher

who thinks he can hit, isn't it?" Spike was not over-sympathetic.

"Yeah, but this Klein's a Jewish boy."

The elder Russell, seated on his bed in the act of removing his shoes and socks from tired feet, looked up quickly. Had his brother been listening to other and older men on the team?

"Oh? He's Jewish, is he?"

"Sure, didn't you know that?" Then after a moment Bob added with authority, "Won't last."

Now Spike knew. It was the same record, the same words and music. He replied quickly, "Why won't he last?"

" 'Cause he's Jewish, that's why. Man, the bench jockeys 'll get him. They'll ride that baby to death, you see if they don't. The pitchers'll dust him off, too. Besides, those Jewish boys can't take it."

His brother's tone and his words irritated Spike. That phrase, he recalled, had jarred on him when Swanson first spoke it. Now it rankled. "What makes you think so, Bobby? How 'bout Newman on the Travelers and Stern with the Crackers and . . ."

"Aw, they're yellow. No guts," announced his brother with the finality of a radio announcer reading a commercial. It was the same line, the same expression, the same verdict Spike had heard previously. "Everyone knows it," continued the younger Russell.

Spike glanced over at his brother. "Why? Who's everyone?"

"Everyone. All the fellows. That throw he made this afternoon on the double steal, remember? It was supposed to be to second; man, it hit the dirt ten feet in front of me."

"Maybe if you'd had that dusting off and fast balls chucked at your noggin all afternoon, you'd be a little nervous, too."

"Maybe. Let's watch him next time. But the boys all say he won't last."

Spike hung his coat on a hanger in the closet, and turned. "He sure can't if the gang doesn't give him some support. D'ja notice when he was chasing that foul fly in the fourth into our dugout, the boys on the bench let him tumble right in. The poor guy like to kill hisself."

"I noticed that. They should have yelled. I yelled."

"So'd I. He never heard—he doesn't know our voices yet, and the coaches were shouting, and everything. But they should have called out in the dugout, those guys sitting there. That's their business. D'ja see, he barked all the skin off his right elbow as it was?"

"Yeah. This ballclub's queer, all right. There are so many cliques and gangs . . . Say, Spike! You know you owe me a nickel."

"By gosh, that's right. So I do."

Since their earliest days in outlaw ball the two always had had a pool into which each one paid a nickel whenever he made an error. They used the money every winter to buy themselves a Christmas dinner at the Andrew Jackson and thus escape Mrs. Hampton's boarding-house on McGavock Street. Back with Charlotte and Savannah in the Sally League that five cents was money. As they earned more money, Bob wanted to increase the ante, but Spike wouldn't hear of such a thing.

"Say, how we stand now?"

Spike drew out his little black notebook and consulted it. In this book he tried every day to write up after the game any information he had obtained that afternoon about the way to play the hitters, details of the pitchers he had faced, facts about their own play around second, and other items pertaining to their trade. He also kept score of their pool, too.

"Why, look here! That's funny! We're exactly

even so far at forty-five cents apiece. Yep, and we're batting close, too. I'm up to one point of you, Bob."

Bob sank into an easy chair and opened up an evening paper. "That's great. Say . . . get a load of this gent." And he began to read from the sports pages.

"We sat on the Brooklyn bench this afternoon for a while during practice and heard lots of good words for the Keystone Kids of Manager Ginger Crane's Drowning Dodgers. If Spike and Bob Russell are as good as the manager and coaches of the team say they are, most of the great second-base combinations of the past should have been in semipro ball. 'Mechanically, this is the best combination I've seen come up,' Crane said yesterday, and Coach Charlie Draper echoed his remarks. 'Me, too, and I've seen some good ones. This Spike is about the best pivot man on a doubleplay I've ever watched.' "

Bob tossed the paper over to his brother, who read the paragraphs.

His face got warm. "Gosh!" he said. Made you solemn, sort of.

Bob became restless. He got up and wandered about the room; then he put on his coat and went out to the elevator, down for a double scoop dish of ice cream before going to bed. Spike stood reading the column again and again. Gosh! It sure scared a fellow, talk like that. Why, that's enough to put the whammy on us, that is!

In ten minutes his brother was back. Bob climbed into bed thinking: Gee, I'm glad I let Spike manage our salary deal last winter. He can handle that MacManus all right. Why, he could even manage this ballclub, Spike could.

Yes, the second base combination of the Dodgers was still working; but the remainder of the club was rapidly sliding down hill. The laughter and jokes of the clubhouse, the free and easy smoothness of their play in spring training had gone. No one wisecracked any more; no one made hot foots or played tricks. Now they were tense and tight, and even Raz grew silent as the season went on into the torrid heat of mid-July and the team sank gradually into sixth place. When a team is in sixth the dressing room loungers, the actors and celebrities, bother it no more. They abandoned the Dodgers to follow the Pirates and the Cards in their struggle for the lead.

Meanwhile, Ginger Crane's desperate attempts to avert disaster had little success. Now his hunches were hunches and nothing more, wild stabs backed by no reasoning, moves made in the hope of changing their luck and finding the right combination to stop their downward slide in the second division. Things looked blacker than an umpire's heart.

"Shoot!" said the manager, in reply to a sportswriter's query just before their first game after returning to Brooklyn. "Shoot! What does it matter who I pitch today? If you don't give a pitcher more than three hits a game, he can't be expected to win for you."

"The boys haven't been hitting recently," said the sportswriter.

"I'll say! We can't seem to buy ourselves a base hit these days."

"It's the hairpins," said Charlie Draper. "We can't find any, so we can't get any two baggers. Since women started cutting their hair short we don't find any hairpins and we don't get any two base hits."

"Let's get some today," said Crane with a burst of his old-time fire. His mouth shut tight. He clapped his hands. "All right now, boys, all right now. Lil' pepper! Take nothing for granted. Lil' pepper today . . . lil' pepper . . ."

They got their hits, too. With the help of these

and a couple of bases on balls and a blooper by Harry Street which dropped dead on the left field foul line with the bags filled, the Dodgers had a four to nothing lead with the game half gone. Directly behind triumph came disaster, as always stalking the second division team.

In the seventh the Cubs got two men on base, and the runner on second tried to score on a single. Karl Case's throw was only a few feet from the plate, but when big Babe Stansworth, the catcher, pivoted to tag the runner sliding around to the rear of the plate, his spike caught in the dirt and his ankle cracked with a snap Spike Russell could hear in the cut-off position behind the box. The team rushed up to him, a stretcher was brought out, and the big chap, writhing in pain, was carried off the field. The Dodgers were left without a first-string catcher to finish out the season and Klein, in the dugout, began nervously fumbling with the buckles on his shin guards.

This incident, the new catcher, the men on second and third, all upset Rog Stinson in the box. He walked the next man, while from the visitors' bench the jockeys howled and on the lines the red-faced coaches joined in the jeering.

"Yeah . . . who's 'at catching now?"

"Hey, Buglenose . . . hold that ball!"

Spike wondered how they had managed to learn the team's nickname for the youngster in such a short time. But he knew things of this sort were part of the rival coaches' business. The boy behind the plate was plainly nervous, Rog was nervous, and the nervousness of the pitcher communicated itself again to the catcher. A ball got away from him and dribbled on the ground back of the plate. He yanked off his mask, twisted rapidly around, pounced on it, juggled the ball, picked it up, and stood there poised to throw.

While the coaches jeered, the runners dashed forward and then darted back to safety, and the rival bench howled with delight. For the moment Klein was saved, but his nervousness was plain for everyone to see. And always from the bench and the coaching lines came that storm of words, of names, of jokes, all directed at the boy there in his catcher's tools.

"Ah there, Buglenose . . ."

"Don't drop that ball, Buglenose . . ."

"Watch out . . . watch out, or you'll be back in the Three I League next week . . ."

Then the batter singled cleanly and two more

runs scored. Now the tieing run was perched on third. A long fly brought it in, and the teams were even at four runs apiece.

The next batter came up with Spike's favorite ball. It was a sizzling grass-cutter well over toward third, a ball that had legs on it, low and fast. Harry, his glove outstretched, stabbed and missed. Spike was there behind the third baseman, waiting for the ball, got it cleanly and burned it home ahead of the heavy, slow baserunner. The huge man on the path was ten feet from home when the ball landed in Klein's hands. So instead of sliding he ran as hard as he could and hurled himself, shoulder forward, at the rookie catcher. The blow knocked Klein spinning, and the ball tumbled from his grasp.

Confusion! Everyone was running. Rog raced for the ball, Harry came charging in from third, and Spike dashed for the plate, too. This was something he wouldn't usually have done. But he snatched the ball from Rog Stinson and ran over to the burly Cub runner, who was picking himself up from the collision and shaking dirt out of his shirt. He slapped the ball on his shoulder.

"He never touched the plate, he never touched the plate!" shouted Spike to the umpire.

From nowhere Crane appeared at his side. For just a second or two his cursing was directed toward the young catcher, and then as he caught the significance of the shortstop's words, he, too, charged Old Stubblebeard, the umpire, with all his fury and all the invective at his command. He shouted, he shrieked, he screamed. His howls drowned out the protests and assertions of the player, the rival manager, and his coaches. For the second time in two days the umpire turned away from the plate, arms folded. But this time his patience was short. Suddenly he turned and pointed toward the dugout.

Ginger refused to budge.

"This'll cost you a hundred dollars," said the umpire. Then Ginger moved. Slowly he moved. He was out of the game.

Too late Cassidy took over the team. The winning run was home and they trooped in to the lockers twenty minutes later, another lead thrown away, another game lost that should have been won, another bitter disappointment, and another cheerless dinner ahead of them. They sat there dispirited and disgusted.

"What time is it?" asked someone finally. "Does anyone know what time it is?"

"Does anyone care?" said a voice. It was typical of their feeling. No one cared.

Crane had for some reason vanished from the room and at least they were thankful to be spared his rasping voice as they slumped down before their lockers.

Tired and discouraged, Spike sat on the bench. Someone touched his shoulder. There was a quiet sentence in his ear. He tried to hear, to understand.

"MacManus wants to see you." He looked up at Bill Hanson, the club secretary.

"Me? Now? Like this?"

"Yeah. You better go right up."

Now what could that mean? Dismissal, probably, or a ticket for Nashville, or a fine at the very least for his raging at the umpire that afternoon. Hang it, he'd defend himself. The man never did touch the plate, never.

He was sure there was something wrong, but he felt almost too tired to think. And he knew Jack MacManus would be in a terrible mood after watching them lose that game. So he was prepared for the worst, prepared also for the owner's red angry face, his abrupt manner. He could see that things had been stormy already that afternoon in the main office.

"Russell! Sit down!" It was a command.

MacManus rose, threw away the stub of a cigar, and lit another. He walked across the room, came back, and reseated himself under the big elk's head on the wall. He started to speak.

Then something hit Spike, hit him hard, knocked all the breath out of him. It was the tense voice of MacManus.

"How'd you like to manage the Dodgers?"

The world went round. He was dizzy. He was insane. He was hearing things. Manager! Manage the Dodgers!

He tried to collect himself, to hold himself down to the chair from which he had been blown by the explosion. Then he heard his own voice, thin, far away.

"Reckon I wouldn't, Mr. MacManus."

That red, freckled face under the sandy hair became redder and redder. "What?" he bellowed. He thumped the desk. "Mean to tell me you'd turn down an opportunity to manage the Brooklyn Dodgers? Here I offer you a chance . . ."

"No, sir, no, Mr. MacManus. You get me wrong. You asked would I *like* to . . . to manage the team. Now . . . and all . . . managing a sixth place club . . . well, that isn't fun, sir."

There was a pause. Then the same hesitating expression came over his broad face that Spike had watched that evening in the Andrew Jackson in Nashville when the five dollar bill had been offered to him. Once again he was ready either to explode with rage or roar with laughter. There was the same moment of tension over the room; then slowly the same grin appeared.

"Spike, by ginger, you're a case! You're the only player who ever got the better of me in a business deal, too. You got an old head on those shoulders, and I believe you can handle this job. What say?"

"Well, sir, it's like this. You've heard the saying—when you sleep on the floor, you can't very likely fall out of bed."

13

The team sat dressing the next morning in the lockers, each player thinking the same thing. He's a good kid; sure he's a good kid. But what will he be like as manager? Will he dish his brother; will he change roomies, or won't he? And what about me? Will I get traded or will he keep me on the team? That's what they were all thinking, all except the second baseman.

Bob was thinking: He's the manager of the Dodgers now; he's Spike Russell, the manager of the Dodgers, the kid that came up from the Nashville Volunteers. He's the manager, Spike is, the best guy who ever lived. Gosh, how I wish the Old Lady could have seen this! Wouldn't she be proud!

Then the door opened and MacManus entered with the new manager, the older man's arm in that of the shortstop. Bob looked at his brother, suddenly realizing that his shoulders had filled out. He's broader and stronger; that's why his ball is steaming in there, why he's getting those extra bases on his hits. There were new lines in his face, lines Bob had never seen there before, and a new seriousness there, too. Now Mac-Manus was talking, talking slowly and calmly, not in the least in his usual vein.

"Of course all you men know there's been an unsatisfactory situation here for some time, and I . . . that is, we . . . that is, the management . . . think the club can go further under a new manager. We're making this change therefore, and we hope you'll back it up with everything you've got." He hesitated, looking at Spike in his monkey suit, standing by his side. "Guess that's about all." He stuck out a big paw. "Spike, good luck! Everyone upstairs is behind you." He turned and walked from the room.

Spike was alone with them. He stood for a minute glancing at the players grouped on the benches or squatting on the floor or leaning against the lockers in the rear; at Roy Tucker with his friendly, honest expression; at Fat Stuff and McCaffrey; at Karl Case, a scowl on his dark, handsome face; at Klein, the black-haired rookie, a catcher's mask under one arm; at Razzle, standing negligently to one side; at Draper and Cassidy, the coaches; at Harry Street and Swanny; and last of all at his kid brother, the best guy who ever lived, the best pivot man in the leagues. Somehow the look on Bob's face gave him courage to go on, to begin, to speak. He raised his head and stuck out his chin.

"I've just been made manager, as you know, and I'll do the best I can; but any success will come—must come, from you guys. It's your show from now on. We all know what the situation here was, what it's been like on this club, and many of us were unhappy. You can't play good ball when you feel that way. We know what the trouble was, no need to go into that. From now on we've got to pull together. This crowd must turn into a real team. From now on no one is working for himself. We're all working for all of us. When you do that, a team has something solid.

"We'll play a little different type of baseball; maybe I've been brought up in a different kind, and of course I expect to play the system I know best. We're not going to fight the umps or the other teams any more. Let's us win ballgames, not arguments. We aren't going to get into rhubarbs with every team in the league. In every one we've been in our club has become disorganized; we've all got mad and lost the game, like that blow-up at Boston the other day where Elmer forgot to cover first. I b'lieve players do better when they keep cool, when they don't lose their heads."

He paused, trying to think of his next point.

Why, he's older, he's grown older, thought Bob. Here I've been living with him, rooming with him all summer, and never noticed it until just now. He's ten years older than he was this time last year. He was growing older right under my eyes and I never realized it. How's that for being dumb?

"I'm manager now, and you won't maybe know how to act. To hell with all that! I'm a ballplayer just the same. I'm out there going through the motions, same as the rest of you. If any of you have anything to say, say it; if you have anything you want to get off your chest, let's thrash it out right here in the clubhouse."

Once again he paused, thinking hard and

trying to phrase his sentences so they wouldn't hurt.

"Now we all know some of us haven't been keeping in shape the way you should. Want you to realize one thing: when you do this, you're hurting all the other men on the club. It isn't just MacManus or the stockholders you hurt when you go out at night. It's us, all of us. That's what I mean when I say in the future we must be a team that pulls together, not an individual record team. I'm sick myself of this whispering stuff in corners.

"I don't hardly think we've been giving enough, either. Oh, sure, I know, you come out and give all you got on the field; I know that. But the point is, if you stay out all night or if you're in your room in the hotel playing gin-rummy 'til three-four in the morning, you just can't . . . you just haven't got it once you get onto the field. That's all going to stop. Anyone who feels he must get loose once in a while, come see me. O.K. I'll give you late permission."

Hang it, thought Bob, the guy's got it. He's really got it! He could see the effect of his brother's words on the team. They were easier now, less tense. Gosh, thought Bob, what a fellow he is, that Spike!

"Now I'm not going to make any radical changes or shake-up in this ballclub. It only needs to hustle. Baseball, as you all know, is played in fractions; fractions of a second, fractions of an inch. I realize I'm not telling you anything; you all know this, especially those of you who've been in the game lots longer'n I have. But seems to me we haven't been hustling; we've been thinking about this or that, about the cut in the meal allowance or how much we lost in that poker game last night or who's running today at Belmont. I want us all to be thinking about who's hitting for them in the seventh instead of who's running in the seventh at Jamaica. Keep on missing signals the way some of us have lately, and we'll all be back seeing the folks at home sooner than we expected.

"From now on I want hustle and more hustle. I want everyone on this club to run out everything to first, whether they think they can beat the throw or not. Yes, and that means all of you pitchers, too. Rats and Elmer and all the rest of you. You gotta presume the fielder's gonna boot that ball. Other day over in Cinci we dropped an important game that shoved us down into sixth place. Why? 'Cause a pitcher started toward first on a hard hit ground ball with his bat in his hand. The shortstop muffed it and threw wild, and he'd been safe if he'd hustled. He didn't hustle and he was out, and we lost the winning run right there when Klein tripled. He was out, and that's out, too, on this club from now on. When you get a single, I expect you to take that turn at first and go on until you see you can't make it. If you can't, O.K., dig in those spikes and hustle back to the bag. But if the fielder so much as bobbles the ball, keep going and you'll be in there. And you won't get a bawling-out if a perfect throw nails you, either. I want you to take chances. You never reach second if you run to first and stop.

"Now there's certain things on this club that's annoyed us all, you and me and everybody. I'm gonna put a stop to 'em. One is morning practice. We been practicing mornings lately, and I think maybe it hurt more than it helped. Maybe we've all got a little stale. 'Nother thing, about the meal allowance. It was cut from six bucks to four bucks this summer, and for some of you big eaters I realize that's not enough. If the other teams in our league get six, we oughta get six, too. We won't have any more of this getting up to eat breakfast together at nine o'clock, either. You come down when you like, jes' so long as it's a reasonable hour. I'm glad to say Mr. MacManus sees things this way, and has agreed to put the meal allowance back where it was."

Man, is he smart! Is that guy smart! They've all been beefing about that meal allowance for the last two months. That coming down to breakfast on the button hurts, too. It's those grudges against the management that burn up ballplayers, that are worse than a two-thousand-dollar cut in salary, thought Bob. Yessir, he's really smart, starting off like that. Looking over the room, he could watch them relax and settle back, see the relief on every face.

So, I'm not fired or traded; he's not shaking everyone up; he's not trying to show his authority right off; he's not sending me back to Montreal. O.K., let's us all go out for this kid, they seemed to be saying to themselves.

"I guess that's about all. For now. This isn't a second division club, and I know if you'll hustle for me we can go places . . . Oh, yes, one more thing. I realize how it upsets a man not to know when he's due to pitch. From now on we'll have a regular schedule. A man'll rest one day after pitching. He'll run and run hard the next day chasing flies. Then he'll throw a little the next day and be ready to pitch if I want him either the fourth or the fifth day. Is that understood? Everyone will take their turn pitching batting practice, too. Raz . . . you'll go in today."

Razzle, leaning against a locker in the back of the room, straightened up and replied hastily. "Yeah, but you know I don't never aim to pitch batting practice, Spike."

It was the first time one of them had addressed the new manager, and the initial contact was a refusal, almost insubordination. As the star of the team's hurling staff, Razzle had never been forced to pitch batting practice by Ginger Crane. The others took their regular turn save the prima donna of the pitchers.

A bench creaked in the stillness. No one spoke, for everyone was watching to see what would happen. Raz stood motionless. He looked at the new manager. The new manager looked back with a steady hardness that Bob had never seen before on the face of his brother.

What'll he say? What'll he do now?

His voice was calm. "Razzle, from now on you'll take your turn out there with the rest. And you'll . . . pitch . . . batting practice . . . today."

Somewhere in the rear another bench creaked

as someone leaned forward to see what the big pitcher would do. He hesitated, astonished, dazed for a moment, his mouth open. Then he slapped his glove.

"O.K., Spike," he said.

A kind of murmur went round the crowded room. Say! Maybe this kid, this rookie manager, isn't going to be so soft after all.

14

Winning Spike's opener as manager of the Dodgers was important. They won it decisively. Winning a doubleheader on his first afternoon in charge was better still. They won those two games as a team, as a unit, something they hadn't been lately. Now we've got a manager, everyone seemed to be thinking. Now we've got a real manager; now we'll go places.

It was the rookie, Klein, whose lusty two bagger won the opener in the ninth and who, with the help of his keen-witted manager, saved the second game. The boy was good. He had a pair of shoulders behind his bat and back of his throws. He had more ginger than old

Stansworth. He kept the pitchers alert by the manner in which he pegged the ball back to them. Also he had a head, and that day he showed he could use it in the pinches. The pinch came in the ninth of the second game, the sort of thing that often happens in a ballgame. Everything goes right, everything breaks your way—up to a point. Then nothing clicks; the play that worked a few innings before doesn't come off; the player who made a wonderful stop the previous inning lets a ball through his legs or misses a signal in a crisis.

The Dodgers were on their toes for the new manager; they were playing as a team, giving everything they had, and for seventeen long innings were on top every minute. Then with a three run lead young Rog Stinson weakened in the ninth. While the huge crowd watched intently, the Cubs, with the top of their batting order crowding the plate, got men on first and third with no one out.

Shrieks and cries came from the stands. "Take him out . . . take him out . . . take him out . . ." The cruel, relentless yell of the mob, the mob that can manage a ballclub from the bleachers better than any manager on the field.

The roar grew, for the fans wanted that game as much as the team.

Would Spike call on old Fat Stuff?

The veteran in the bullpen, pretending as usual not to hear the call, threw in a few extra warm-up pitches and then waddled across to the box where Spike and Klein were waiting. It was the first time Klein had caught the old timer.

"Hope you're not one of these pitch-out catchers!"

"No, sir," replied the boy. "You get that ball in there and I'll take my chances with the men on bases."

"O.K., Fat Stuff! O.K., Jocko! Let's go," said Spike, slapping the pitcher on the back.

The team and the batter and the whole ballpark settled into that ninth inning tension, the tenseness that spells drama, that comes when the shadows hang over the diamond, when a tight one hangs in the balance. A hit, a throw, a close decision, and there goes your ballgame. That afternoon the tenseness was the more acute because of the young manager. Out in deep short he kicked nervously at the pebbles in the dirt.

"Strike one!" cried the umpire.

A roar went up with his hand, and all over the diamond came the chatter, especially from second base. A ball. Another strike. Fat Stuff was working carefully and confidently on the batter, teasing him with a low one. Two and two.

Suddenly on the next pitch the man on first broke. Spike, in deep short, was ready. He half expected a steal and came charging into the cut-out position behind the box, anxiously watching Klein receive the ball, half seeing the umpire's hand go up as the batter swung fiercely. How would the youngster react? Would he become the typical rookie, holding the ball for fear the man on third would dash home? Or would he crack and throw the ball into center field?

The double steal with men on first and third is one of the hardest plays to prevent. The prevention falls almost entirely on the catcher. In half a second or less he must decide whether to throw to third and hand the other man second base. This was the moment, this was the test. This might make him or break him.

With one glance over his left shoulder at third, the catcher took the hard way. He pegged high at Spike in the cut-off position, just as the man on third broke for home. The manager caught the ball shoulder high and burned it back to the plate, nabbing the runner by yards. Klein tagged him as he slid in, jumped aside, and shot the ball to second where the base-runner was four feet off the bag toward third. Bob, waiting, slapped the ball on him for the second out.

A roar broke out all over the stands, and Spike, turning, saw his brother toss his glove back onto the grass. It was the third out, for the man at the plate had swung on the third strike. They had made a triple play. The game was won.

They came charging in from the field while the crowd stood roaring above. Hands slapped at them as they rushed under the dugout and into the locker room.

"That's heads-up ball there, Buglenose," said old Fat Stuff affectionately.

"That's the angle, Jocko."

"Nice work, Buglenose, nice work there! That's keeping your eyes peeled."

Everyone had a good word for the rookie except Karl Case, who sat beside his locker muttering. "Howsat for luck? This kid breaks into a triple play his first month in the league! I never been in on a triple play and I been in the majors eleven years. Howsat for luck?"

Everyone else was happy; happy, loose, and warm. The warmth came from inside, not from the exercise in the hot July sunshine.

Now we've got a manager, we'll go places. We've got a manager and a catcher, too. Stansworth was so old he wasn't getting down to the low ones half the time.

"Boy," said Spike, "you like to burn my hands off on that cut-off play. You can throw all right, and you get 'em off quick, too. O.K., gang. Train leaves Pennsylvania at eight-thirty. We gotta hustle. Don't forget to take your jackets. It gets cold out on that lake front there . . ."

They piled into the train and assaulted the dining car. An hour and a half later they returned in twos and threes. Spike and the coaches were together in a drawing room working over the Reds' batting order. As usual, Red Allen turned to the evening newspaper and a crossword puzzle. Case and Street and Swanny, the card players, broke open a pack. The door of their compartment was ajar as the young catcher passed by on his way from the diner. He paused a moment in the doorway.

"Nice work, Buglenose, nice work on that cut-off play," said Swanny. The rookie stood leaning against the doorway while Harry Street pulled a suitcase onto their laps and Swanny began to shuffle the cards.

"What's that?" asked the rookie. "One down and four up?"

"Yeah."

"How's for letting me in on it? I played that all over the Middle West these last years."

Swanny looked at Case and Case glowered at Swanny. There was a moment of silence which some would have noticed. But the young catcher, feeling himself a part of the team, exhilarated by the warmth of their approval, by his play in the last inning, did not perceive Case's glowering glance, nor understand the hesitating silence that followed his request. On a ballclub the rookies all play cards together and the veterans have their own game. The old timers usually have a higher stake and don't want to take money the youngsters can't afford to lose. For a minute or so no one answered the young catcher.

Then Swanny replied, "Why, sure! What the hell! Here, sit over beside me." And he made room for the youngster.

Two hours later Spike was turning in, tired but happy. Manager at last, with two games to his credit, and the team really taking hold. Being manager wasn't so bad at that! Unable to sleep, he lay thinking over the game and especially the last inning, feeling the satisfaction of finding that hole behind the plate well filled, looking ahead to the trials of the road trip in the July heat, half listening all the while to the roaring of the train and the occasional voices of passers-by in the corridor.

Then a familiar voice came to him. It was Karl Case. Karl, as usual, was complaining.

What's biting that guy now, thought Spike. He got four hits this afternoon; he ought to be happy.

"Yeah, well, we had no business letting a kid like that in the game. Anyhow, who ast him? Nobody ast him, that's who ast him. He shoulda minded his own affairs. The fresh young Jewboy! He butts in and takes all our dough. Sixty-six bucks it cost me, the nervy busher . . ."

He moved along the corridor, still grumbling. The door of his compartment slammed shut.

15

From that moment Case had it in for young Klein. Karl Case, the wickedest bench jockey in the league, was by no means the most popular man on the club. His tongue was an asset when turned on their adversaries, a liability when he went after a teammate, which he often did. Once he got "on a man" he could be really mean.

To be sure, everyone on the club addressed the rookie catcher as Buglenose. That was his nickname, his name on the bench and in the clubhouse, just as Fat Stuff and Spike and Rats were nicknames. There was comradeship in it, affection almost. After the card game on the train, however, there was a note in Karl's voice which made the young catcher look up flushing when the swarthy outfielder spoke to him. Naturally Case didn't miss this sign.

"Hey there, Buglenose, lemme get a cut at that-there grapefruit." Or, "Looka, Buglenose, save me a rap for a change, will ya?"

At first only a few of them noticed his tone. But by that sudden reddening the rookie catcher confessed he had felt it from the start.

Next came the clash, the clash that was probably inevitable, given that incident on the train and the temperaments of the two men, yet damaging to the team at that critical moment in the season. Perhaps had it all happened in private the trouble would have blown over. Flare-ups of that kind often help settle a team that is trying to find itself. A manager makes the men shake hands and get it all off their minds. Case would then have forgotten the loss of his sixty-six dollars and, more important still, the injury to his vanity when, as the best poker player on the team, he was taken over by a rookie from Rochester.

Unfortunately the whole thing took place in the worst spot of all—on Forbes Field where the Pirate coaches missed nothing. It happened before the game and during practice where those old-timers on the Pitt bench observed its full significance. Coaches make it their business to use every available weapon.

The Dodgers were at batting practice. Case swaggered to the plate, took his cuts, and on the last ball laid one down just inside the first base line, a bunt that was fair by inches. Klein, the rookie catcher, instinctively dashed for the ball. Case saw his chance and took it. As the two thundered toward first, nearing the ball, Klein leaned over to pick it up, and as he did so the outfielder charged through, stepping on his bare hand and at the same time cracking him on the thigh with his rising knee.

The two men tumbled to the grass, rolled over, picked themselves up, and went for each other. There was a moment when they stood face to face, the hot-tempered Case spoiling for a fight as revenge for his hurt pride, ready to receive a punch or give one; Klein wringing his hand, uncertain. The second was there; it came and passed. The punch was never delivered.

"Back to yer tools, Buglenose. And the next time clear out of my way, see?"

This even reached Bob on second base who caught the sneer in Case's tone. He watched them stand, faces a few inches apart, saw the catcher still shaking his bleeding hand turn slowly away and move back toward the plate. As the rookie leaned over to pick up his mask, it flashed on Bob. Why, the guy can't take it!

Back on the bench the Pirate coaches observed the incident with pleasure and instantly filed it for future use. The exact moment to use it came two hours later.

The Dodgers were behind that afternoon, and toward the end of the game had a three run lead to overcome. In the eighth they had loaded the bases, with two out, when the rookie catcher shuffled to the plate. Suddenly, without warning, the barrage broke in full force from the Pirate bench.

"Hey! Hey there, Buglenose . . ."

"Watch out, Jew-boy, watch out or you'll get yerself kilt up there!"

"Oh, you Buglenose!"

"Danny, show up that kike. Let him look at your fast one. He won't dare offer at it."

The last shot made the boy wince. He betrayed his emotion by a quick turn of his head toward the opposing bench. His bat waved menacingly but this was merely an act. That shot got home and the Pitt coaches knew it immediately. So did the scattered substitutes along the dugout seat who joined in the pursuit. The bench jockeys were off in full cry.

"Better duck, Buglenose, better duck . . ."

"Watch yerself, Buglenose, watch yerself there, or he'll pare that beak off'n ya!"

The pitcher threw in a strike. The bat never moved from Klein's shoulder. From the opposing dugout the torrent of noise increased. On the coaching lines behind third Spike saw what was happening, cupped his hands and shouted, trying to encourage the red-faced rookie at the plate. Again the pitcher tossed in a fast ball. The batter leaned but didn't offer. Once again the bat remained in his hands, motionless.

"Get your bat offa your shoulders, Jocko. You can't expect to hit if you don't swing at 'em." Spike yelled as loud as he could, but his voice was lost in the clamor of abuse from the dugout of the home team.

The next pitch was wide. Then another ball, a low one at which the batter offered feebly and fouled into the stands. Then came a third strike, a fast one, dead across the plate.

"You're out!"

The boy's bat never moved. The inning was

over and with it the Dodgers' chance for that important game.

Significant things about a ballclub can't be told in black and white. No sportswriter mentioned the incident the following morning. But news of this kind travels fast in the baseball grapevine, and they were all waiting for Klein in Cincinnati, the next stop.

That rookie with the Dodgers, boy by the name of Klein, they all say he can't take it!

So they were waiting, the same hard-voiced coaches on the lines, the same cruel jockeys in the dugout. His batting slumped. In one game he failed to hit the ball out of the infield or reach first.

The attitude of the team began to change. Say, whazza matter? Can't the guy take it or what? This-here game is no place for anyone who can't take it!

Case was after him incessantly, and Bob, ever talkative, joined in. So did others. Their voices now were no longer tinged with warmth; there was a change in their tones. By the time the club reached Chicago, the rookie was making mistakes, bungling plays, even getting his signs crossed.

With the same set-up on which a triple play

had been made on Spike's first afternoon as manager—men on first and third and nobody out—the shortstop signaled Klein to throw to second should a steal be attempted. The youngster got flustered, mixed everything up, and instead threw at Razzle in the box. Raz had his head half turned toward second, the throw went past, past Bob into center field, and another game was gone.

That evening the Keystone Kids lay in twin beds on the eighteenth floor of the Netherlands Plaza, waiting for sleep and thinking all the time of the lost opportunity of that afternoon. From below the roar of the traffic came to their ears.

"Why, Spike, he's so doggone nervous he don't know what city he's in."

"Yeah . . . he's nervous all right."

"I'll say! Well, I knew from the start he hadn't got it."

"You knew nothing!"

"I knew he'd never make the grade. Not in this league. Jew-boys can't last in the big time."

For almost the first time in his life the older brother felt annoyed at the younger one. What's he mean? Who's he been blatting to? He tried not to show his annoyance.

"What do you mean, they can't last?"

"They can't, that's all."

"Aw, you been listening to Swanny. And Case. That guy's a troublemaker. He ain't charging the fences or standing up to the hurlers with the loose pitching habits the way he used to, either. I wish he'd been traded last spring like Ginger Crane tried to."

"No, you're dead wrong there, Spike. You're wrong this time and Case is right. We want no quitters on this-here club. If a guy can't take it, he hasn't any place in baseball."

"Well, sure, I'd agree to that. But if you and Case and the boys get on him all the time, why, any rookie would crack. What's biting Case, anyhow?"

"What's biting him? That poker game. Didn't you hear about that?"

"No. What? When?"

"Coming out from New York the first night. Case and Swanny and a couple of the old-timers were getting down to their game of one-and-four, when along comes this fresh busher and invites himself into it. You know, Spike, no one but a fresh Jew-boy would have the gall to do a thing like that. The rookies play their game and the old-timers play theirs. But this brassy kid has to butt in and walk away with their cash."

"Aha! So that's it, is it? That's what started the whole thing. How much did Case drop?"

"Sixty-six bucks. Listen, Spike! You know what I think? I b'lieve the boys would go better with another catcher."

"Don't talk to me about another catcher. I haven't got another catcher, you know that. You know you don't buy catchers at the Five and Ten in July. Stansworth's out for six weeks. This guy Kenny is too fat and too old to use outside the bullpen. Mac wired me there's a boy coming down from Montreal tomorrow or the next day. He batted two thirty-five so far this season. Two thirty-five! Anyhow, if he batted four thirty-five, I still wouldn't give up on Jocko Klein. He's a good kid and he's one swell ballplayer, and he could be a catcher, too, if only you guys, you and Case and Swanny, would give him a chance. That tightwad Case . . ."

"Give him a chance! Who ever gave you and me a chance? We got no chances given us. We took our chances; we went in and grabbed 'em off. Remember, Spike, remember how we jumped into outlaw ball in that old Tobacco League? Remember how we both braced Peterson that time at the Charlotte ballpark, and how he laughed at us, and how we showed him that day we had the goods? Remember Savannah, and those games when we pulled up from last place? Remember . . ."

"Yes, of course I remember. I remember no one ever gave it to us like you boys are giving it to this fella. No one ever called us a couple of quitters all day long. That's what you boys are doing to him. No, sir, I can't see a good kid ruined. I'm not giving up on him—even if you are."

There! It was out. Yet once out, he wished he hadn't said it. Ordinarily he would never have said it to Bob, but the strain was telling. He was upset and tired. He had been presented with a situation which he had never faced and never seen Grouchy handle. What would Grouchy do? He wished with all his heart he hadn't said what he did or said it just that way in just that tone to Bob, the best guy who ever lived. Somehow it made the space between the two beds wider.

"Aw . . . what's the use? He's a Jew-boy. He ain't an American."

The space became wider still.

"Whaddya mean he ain't an American? He was born in K.C. and raised there, went to school there, same as you were raised in Charlotte." The gap was wider and wider. "Say, whaddya mean? He works here, on this club; he plays ball same as you do. Where d'you get that stuff, he ain't an American? He's just as much an American as you are."

Bob became irritatingly disagreeable. "Aw, well . . . anyhow, it's different."

Maybe if they hadn't both been tired, maybe if it hadn't been Cincinnati in the heat, maybe if the traffic hadn't drummed continually in their ears, maybe if they'd won that afternoon instead of losing, maybe then it would never have happened. The gap would have closed and they would have remained the Keystone Kids.

Spike picked up the challenge in his brother's tone. "Yeah? How's it different?"

"It's different, that's all. And you know it's different. Jews aren't athletes; they never were. They can't take it, they're gonna crack, they always crack . . ."

"Oh, you make me tired. A Jew's like anyone else. Some of 'em can't take it, some can."

"Listen, I'm telling you, Spike . . ."

"Nuts to that! You been getting this from those beefers, Karl Case and . . ."

"See here, Spike! I'm only trying to help you. Of course, if you're gonna be obstinate about it . . . if you wanna split the team in two . . . just keep on . . . you're doing fine."

Obstinate! That was the word that set him off. Obstinate!

He sat up. He turned toward his brother. "Now just one thing! We better understand each other. I'm running this here team. As long as I'm the manager, I don't need any help from Swanny or Karl or you or anyone else, and as long as I *am* in charge, I'm not going to see a good boy like Klein torn to pieces by a bunch of snarling bench jockeys. Do you get me? You guys play ball and leave me pick the line-up. That goes for everyone, you, too. I don't want to hear any more about this. No more. Not a word."

He sank down suddenly. There was no sound from the other bed. Then Bob turned over. His back was plainly visible. Spike turned over, too, and there they lay, quiet, awake, unable to sleep. It was not the heat, nor the noise of the traffic below, not even throwing away that game that kept both the Keystone Kids awake all night.

16

St. Louis under the Missouri sun, and no fun either. Red Allen was at bat, and from the bench came Bob's staccato cry, "Shake it up there, Red; wake up those bats, big boy." After waiting for three balls and fouling half a dozen pitches, Allen popped up. It was a high fly to short, an easy out. But the big first baseman, refusing to quit, took his turn round the bag at full speed and started with all his strength for second. He was nearly there when the ball settled into the shortstop's glove. Case, always ready to sneer, leaned down toward Bob on the long bench. In between them sat Jocko Klein, his dark eyes solemn as he looked across the diamond.

"D'ja see that there, Bob? That's baseball, kid. D'ja see him run out that fly ball?"

"Sure did. There's a ballplayer, what I mean, in there trying every minute."

"Uhuh. We could do with a few more on this club," rejoined Case.

"I'll say. O.K. O.K., now, Roy. Shake up those bats. Let's us get some hits now."

The batting order had been changed by Spike in an endeavor to get the team moving and Klein followed Tucker. He went over to the bat rack, wiped his hands on a towel, and stepped from the dugout while Roy walked up to the plate. He stood motionless, his arms well out like all free arm hitters. On the first pitch he swung hard and missed.

"The big one left, Roy, the big one left," yelled Bob.

Timing the pitch perfectly, Tucker caught the next ball on the fat of his bat and drove it through the box for a clean single. From the coaching lines back of third Spike clapped his hands as his catcher came to bat.

"O.K., Jocko boy. O.K., boy. Make him pitch to you alla time, Jocko, alla time, boy." His voice was lost in the sudden noise from the

Cardinal dugout when they saw the rookie step to the plate.

"Oh, Jocko, look out now! Don't let him hurt you up there."

"Watch out, you yeller Jew-boy, watch out or he'll burn them letters offa yer chest."

The boy at the plate looked at a ball, swung hard at a curve and fouled it off, then attempted a bunt. It was a sorry attempt, a kind of half-hearted try. The ball sailed gently into the air, slowly enough and high enough so the pitcher could step quickly forward and grab it, so slowly that Tucker had a chance to slide safely back to first. Klein returned disconsolately to the dug-out. From above came the voice of a fan.

"Hey there, Klein, is that the way they teach you to bunt in Brooklyn? Is that how they teach you?"

Karl Case, the next man, hit with authority. It was a single to left, advancing Tucker. So there were men on first and second with two out. Karl stood nonchalantly on the bag, exchanging caps with Cassidy, mopping his dark face with his sleeve, grinning unpleasantly at the dugout and the rookie catcher. The veteran was pleased with himself. Now if only the rest of the club played this kind of ball. . . .

The first delivery was a pitchout. Suddenly the catcher made a snap throw, low, hard, to the left corner of first base. Although Karl slid back with outstretched arms, he was cut down and the side retired. Four men up, two clean singles, and not a runner past second base. Karl returned to the bench grumbling, reached for a towel, and muttered half to himself, "If that bird only knew how to bunt, this'd never have happened."

They trooped past the jeering fans above, and into the dressing room, hot, dirty, tired, and disappointed.

This can't continue, thought Spike, things can't go on like this. I must do something. I'm the manager. I've got to act now.

That evening after dinner he knocked at Klein's room. Fat Stuff, who had been put with him as a steadying influence, was out, and the dark-eyed boy himself opened the door.

"Oh! Hullo, Spike. Come in." His tone was hardly overcordial. Spike stepped inside. It was the usual ballplayer's bedroom; newspapers on the floor, an opened suitcase on a rack, another suitcase on a chair, several magazines on the table beside the telephone. The manager sat on the bed, while the rookie looked over from across the room, eyeing him defensively, saying nothing.

Now Grouchy, how would Grouchy handle this kid, thought Spike, anxious not to make a mistake. He began cautiously. "Well, Jocko, things don't look so good for our side, do they?"

The boy seemed relieved. He agreed. But he said nothing as he nodded. Silence once more.

"Nope," Spike continued, more because he had to keep on than because he knew how to proceed. "No, we ain't clicking. Grouchy Devine—you know Grouchy, he was my old manager on the Vols—he always used to say when things are darkest, that's when a manager has to be able to yank his club out of a hole." He paused. Maybe he would get some help. No help came.

Instead the catcher, seated on the stiff chair across the room, glowered at him sullenly. The embarrassing silence continued. Boy, we aren't getting anywhere fast. This won't do, thought Spike. He looked at the rookie catcher. "What seems to be the trouble, what's the trouble do you think, Jocko? I'm asking you."

The black eyes spoke volumes but the lips never moved. Still that sullen look hovered over his face. This was even more difficult than Spike had imagined, and he had foreseen plenty of trouble. But he persisted. "Seems to me . . . kinda . . . as if . . . well, as if the club's not together. I felt it was going real good right after Ginger Crane left. Now they've slumped again." Silence. "Haven't they?"

The boy assented but nothing more. He still refused to talk. Gosh, thought Spike, this is sure a tough one. What would Grouchy do next?

"Jocko, I'm not so old myself, but I been in this game quite some time. Baseball is two things for my book—ability and confidence. You got the ability all right; you showed us all that last month. You can throw, you can hit, you have a bean and you use it. But your confidence is all washed up. What's the trouble, boy?"

Klein shook his head in a gesture that could mean anything. But talk he would not.

"What's the matter?" Spike was getting annoyed. He knew he should above all keep control of himself; yet he was tired, and the stubborn persistence of the rookie catcher was upsetting. "Listen, Jocko, what's eating you, anyhow?"

"I . . . we . . . the club . . . I dunno." He was trying now, he tried but he couldn't go on. The thing was far too deep and too bitter, and he was unable to let himself go. "You wouldn't understand . . ."

"Jocko-boy, le's have it straight. I'm your friend. I got all kinds of confidence in you. I know you have the stuff, see, otherwise you'd be sitting in Elmira right this minute."

The boy was grateful. He tried once more, he stuttered and stopped. "Case . . . it's Case, and your brother . . ."

Spike wanted to be patient, to understand. Yet he found difficulty as a ballplayer in comprehending these things. "Why, now, the boys don't mean anything. You know how they are. They'll needle their own sister if it gets under her skin. That's baseball. You know that."

Klein shook his head in despair. "Spike, seems like you just can't understand."

"Jocko, tell me, what's the matter? Why can't you take it? When did this hit you first?"

"You wanna know?" He leaned suddenly forward toward him. "You wanna know? All right, here goes. I'll tell you . . . only you won't understand. . . ."

17

It came when I was . . . le's see . . . I must have been eight or nine years old. We lived with my grandfather, me and my cousins, a bunch of us kids, so naturally we always played together and stuck together. We never got to know other kids very well. Then one day I was playing alone in the street, and another boy from down the road came by and said, 'Hey, are you a kike? Are you a kike?' "

The words poured out. Klein had no trouble talking now as he told the story of himself which was the story of his people. " 'Are you a kike?' And I said, 'Am I a kite? Of course I'm not a kite.' 'Ha,' he said, 'I guess you don't know what a kike is.' So I went inside and found my mother. 'Ma,' I said, 'what's a kike, what is it?' My mother, she looked at me a long, long while.

"Finally she told me. She told me lots, what was behind us Jews, back, way, way back, Spike, back so far you wouldn't understand, back thousands of years. 'Son,' she said, 'you've got to know some time; you might as well know right now. This is what we're up against, all of us, what we've been up against, what we've had to fight since the start of things.' And she told me, told me everything, a lot you wouldn't hardly realize, a lot I couldn't explain. How my grandfather Klein escaped from Vienna, and his grandfather was chased out of Poland, and . . . and . . ."

"No . . . sure . . . yes . . ." Spike hardly knew what to say, how to answer. What could you say? What could you answer?

"I know what you're gonna tell me. Oh, but you Jews, you're so pushing, you're always shoving. I know, I heard. No one but a Jew . . . only a Jew would act that way, like that. It's true, too. We have to. How could we live if we hadn't done that? It comes from a thousand years of torture and hate against us. I don't expect you to understand. Lemme explain so you will, maybe; lemme see if I can show you what I mean, Spike. Now take St. Loo. We're in a tough town; here's where the fans are really tough. You know how it is in St. Loo in a close series; you go off the field together, you stick with the boys or else you may get yourself clipped on the back by some fan with a pop bottle. See, that's the way it is with us Jews; we've stuck together for preservation. It's deep in us, in our blood. Like a team alone fighting the stands full of fans in a strange town. Funny thing; folks don't like the way we act; then they make us act the way we do. Spike, I guess you'll never understand, I guess no one who hasn't been through it will understand. . . ."

Spike understood. Dimly, feebly, he saw through the words into all that lay back of them. Now he nodded. Now he was doing the nodding and the rookie catcher was talking.

"No, no. You can't, ever. I guess it's too hard. I guess I can't explain. Wait a minute. Look, d'ja ever read poetry?"

Read poetry! Oh, migosh! The question made Spike uncomfortable, and he was uncomfortable enough as it was. He shifted on the edge of the bed. What was this guy, anyhow? A ballplayer reading poetry! There were men who read comics, and a good many who read the racing sheets, and some who read magazines, and a few who read detective stories, and one or two like Red Allen who even did crossword puzzles. But books, never, and poetry!

Then for the first time he noticed a half-opened volume on the dresser. A catcher reading poetry, that's awful bad. This kid must be wacky or something. That's bad, that's really bad. Why, if the boys ever get hold of this, they'll skin his hide off'n him. Lucky he's rooming with old Fat Stuff, a gent that keeps his trap closed. You think you've been round and seen things, yet you're forever running up against something new. Imagine, a catcher reading poetry! Ain't that something!

The boy went on. "I happened to read it in there. Like this, it goes like this. 'A river runs between these men and me . . . a river of blood and time.' "

Spike broke in. He tried to interrupt. "Yeah, that's right, I guess. Yeah, I getcha, Jocko. Boy, you really got something there." Better just kid him along a little, let him work it off; maybe do him good.

But the boy went right on, paying no attention, his voice higher, his black eyes afire.

Gosh, this was terrible. Suppose Fat Stuff opened the door with that kidder, Rats Doyle, right at this minute! Perhaps the poor guy is nuts. Say, maybe we drove him nuts, like what's-his-name, that catcher on the Reds who commited suicide several years ago.

" '. . . And we speak to each other across the roar of that river . . . but no more.' " His voice was louder. "Look! I'm a Jew. It's in my blood . . ."

"That's enough!" Spike jumped up from the bed. He walked across to where the boy was sitting taut on the edge of the chair.

"That's enough!" Now he was the manager, he took charge. This must stop; and quickly. "That's enough, that's all of that, Jocko. Listen to me! If you ever pull this-here Jew stuff on me again . . . if you ever do . . . I'll . . . I'll break every bone in your body . . . so help me, Hannah, I will. Don't you ever say those things again, don't you dare. . . ."

"They all say them, or think them. They're against me, everyone, 'cause I'm Jewish."

"Jocko! For the last time! Don't lemme hear you crack like that again, or I'll make you so lame you won't go to bat for a week. I mean it, too. Now listen. You're a good catcher. You've gone all to pieces because these last few weeks Karl Case . . ."

"Yessir, him and your brother and Swanny and Rats Doyle and . . ."

"O.K. Them, too, they've been on you. They been on you good and plenty. D'you think I'm blind? I can see, I can hear, I know what's going on. They been on you; so now you quit, you quit on us cold, on me . . . on the club. You let them bench jockeys get you down. That's the trouble with you Jews. You're up against it, sure; you're up against it plenty, and you don't fight back when you should fight back. You let them guys get you down. There's times, Jocko, when a guy has to fight back. They come to us all, every one of us, like they came to me one afternoon down in Nashville when I saw Mugger Smith carving his initials in my kid brother's legs . . ."

"But, Spike, it's different; y'see, the prejudice . . ."

"Sure, I know there's prejudice on this team, and you're the one to suffer; you're the victim, the one to take it. O.K., only don't you understand you made it worse yourself. Don't you get that? They'd have been prejudiced against you if you'd been a Hottentot or a Turk or a Texas boy who acted same as you did. So now . . ."

"So what? So what? Tell me, what can I do, what should I do . . ."

"Why, stand up to 'em. Don't show 'em they can get to you. Don't quit . . . "

"It's easy for you to talk."

"I know. But I'm the manager of the team. I gotta tell you these things. I hafta smooth out these troubles, that's what managers are for. These boys aren't really wrong guys. Now take my brother; he's an all right sort of a person, he isn't mean. Sure . . ." He saw the protest rise to the other's lips.

"He isn't, hey? Well, he . . ."

"I know; he's wrong on this, but he isn't a mean guy. Only your fear shows through, your fear of his dislike, and Case's. Somehow it builds up their bullying and their bullying builds up your fear of their dislike. Wonder am I saying it so you'll get me? Because now, see, you say like this; I'll never be any good on account I'm Jewish. They realize you feel that way. They know it. Boy, you gotta take it in this game same as you gotta take it in life. Get me? Understand?" He looked down at him. Yes, he was getting it, slowly. He nodded deliberately at the manager standing above him.

"Now don't ever let me hear you spouting that

poetry stuff any more, never. Oh, that's bad, Jocko, that's really bad. I want you. I need you. The team needs you the worst way. Why, we can win if you play like you can; we can go places with this bunch. Once they see you're a scrapper, they'll be for you, all the way. You wait and see."

"Think so? D'you really think so, Spike?"

"I know so. I know my kid brother; I know tnese guys, every one of 'em. Now stay with us. Remember, I'm behind you, all the time. I'm fighting for you. You get in there and fight for yourself. Fight, Jocko, will ya, kid?"

Klein stood up. His short sturdy figure was straight and firm. As he rose the chair fell over back with a clatter. "O.K., Spike, I'll try. I'll give it everything; gimme a chance and I think I'll pull out of this spin."

"Darn right you will. I'm not giving up on you, Jocko. Don't you give up on yourself."

18

Bob guessed where Spike had been the moment he returned to their room that night.

"Well, Spike, how's your young Jewish pal tonight?"

"If he's a pal of mine he's a pal of yours, Bob. We're all playing on the same side, you know."

"No, *sir*." There was conviction in his tone. "No, sir, he's no pal of mine, I'm telling you."

"If you'd only try to understand the guy a little, he might be. And we might become a team, too."

"Hey, what is this? A Lonely Hearts club? I

always thought it was a bunch of ballplayers. Be reasonable, Spike. C'mon now, be reasonable. Be a good fellow; be reasonable about this. You got the whole team against you. What can you expect of a Jew-boy? You better trade him, and the sooner the better, I'd say. No wonder he can't take it; he never will with you a-babying him the way you do."

"First off, I'm not babying him. I'm only trying to make him the catcher of this-here team."

"Well you won't. Make up your mind to that. You better give up on him. You're foolish to string along with him."

"No, sir, I ain't giving up on him, not yet awhile I ain't."

"O.K. You're a sap, that's all."

Bob hung up his trousers and climbed into bed. If he won't take any advice from his own brother, if he won't take any help from me, he won't, that's all. He always was like that, stubborn and obstinate. Once he gets his mind set he's like a North Carolina mule. You just can't do a thing with him. O.K. Let him find out for himself. Let him make a fool of himself if he wants to. I won't help him again, or try to, either.

Spike stood looking out of the window. It hurt

to hear those words but the tone hurt even more; it was a tone his brother had never used before. It hurt also to feel the gap between them widening all the time.

The next afternoon they made a bad slip in the field. Bob was watching Klein, his eyes searching for a sign of weakness in the man behind the plate. With a left-handed pull hitter at bat, Bob ran over to cover second, although Spike had signaled that he would cover the bag. Just as Bob ran over, too, the batter cracked the ball into the slot he vacated, and the runner on second slid home with the winning run.

The following day in St. Louis Spike watched it happen again, realizing bitterly that this difference, this break in their affections, was damaging their play together. It was actually hurting their combination and destroying the understanding and co-ordination which had made them the Keystone Kids; which had brought them from Savannah to Dallas, to the Volunteers in Nashville, and from Nashville to Ebbets Field, Brooklyn.

They were behind 2-1 in a tight game, a game Spike wanted badly. And a game they needed. In the eighth Bob got a base on balls, and when Spike came to the plate, his brother was still on first with one out. Spike managed to work the pitcher into a hole. At three-and-one he put on the hit-and-run sign, and smashed a scorching bounder which would have been behind the runner had Bob not missed the signal. The ball, instead of going through into right field, went directly to the hands of the Card second baseman, who ordinarily on a hit-and-run would have been covering the bag. It was a doubleplay and the end of the Dodgers' chances.

"Doggone, Bob, you messed that up. You lost the signal again . . ." Spike was furious.

"No, no, I saw it O.K., Spike. I saw it but I didn't think you could have meant it."

This only made him the more angry. First, a missed signal, a thing that never used to happen when they were clicking, something at which they always laughed when they saw other men do it. Then worse, Bob's refusal to admit his mistake. For just a second Spike was so upset he wanted to call his brother down, to make an example of him there before the other players, to bench him on the spot, to discipline him so he never again would mess up another sign. But he knew how upset and annoyed he himself was. So he trotted out glumly to his place in the field. At times like these being a manager is no fun.

Gosh, he thought, as he burned the ball over to Red on first. Holy smoke, this thing is affecting us, too. Why, Bobby and me, we can't even play together any more!

19

They sat before the game on the long benches in front of the lockers, and in the middle of the semicircle stood their manager.

This managing a ballclub is beginning to tell, thought Bob, as his brother began to speak. Why don't he chuck that Jewish kid? What's the sense of it? What's the use of making an issue of it, of fighting seven clubs in the race and half your own team, too? It don't make sense. He's just plain stubborn, he always was that way; he never did like to admit he was wrong, never. Sometimes, like when you're holding out for a raise on your contract, that's a mighty valuable thing. Now it's breaking him in two. He can't trade Klein without letting Mac and everyone else know he made a mistake. Well, he'll have to admit it sooner or later.

"Nope," Spike was saying, "the club isn't clicking yet the way it can, the way I hoped it would, but we gotta take time to shake down. I don't ask the impossible of you boys. All I ask is you go out there and hustle. Some of you aren't hustling as you should. That's the chief fault of most ballplayers, seems like, not hustling. Yesterday, Swanny, when you were on first, remember, you jogged down to second on Roy's single. Remember? Their center fielder fumbled and then you broke for third. Lucky the throw was wild. As it was you had to slide in to get there. If you'd been going all out every minute, you might have scored. Case popped up and we were through without a run. That's bad. One more thing. The hitting isn't what it should be, not by any means. A few of you boys aren't hitting as you can; you, Red, and you, Klein, and you, Harry. Never mind. No matter if you go nine times without a hit, get in there the tenth time and grab me that single. It might even win the game. Anyhow it goes in the book, and a hundred is a darn sight better than zero in the hit column. Give me everything you got all the time."

Old Chiselbeak, the locker room attendant, stuck his nose in the door. "Where's Jocko Klein? Hey there, Jocko! Long distance call for you in the office upstairs."

The black-haired boy with the catcher's mitt under his arm uncoiled himself from the floor and went out.

"Roy! Roy Tucker! Shut that door." Spike's voice was curt and sharp, not persuasive as it had been. "Now there's one thing I'd like to get across today with every single man, an' I want everybody to get it straight. This is a team. Perhaps we can't win the pennant, although I haven't written us off yet by any means. But there's one thing we can be, a team that's pulling together. What's that say? Says we're all trying hard out there for each other. Says something else, too. That every man's as good as anyone else, no matter who he is or where he comes from. There's one player on this club you haven't been behind. You all know who it is. You think he's yeller, so you don't give him support on the field. You're watching to see him make mistakes. Case, that's how you got trapped off first the other day. Well, lemme tell you something. He isn't yeller. He's a scrapper.

"Yessir, he's a fighter. He's a fighter and he's fighting something big. He's fighting . . . how shall I say it . . . he's fighting what all of us who aren't Jews have done to all those who are, not just right now, not right here, but for so far back you wouldn't understand. It's what they've had to fight, really, since the start of things."

Around the room heads came slowly up, bodies straightened. He heard Red Allen's mitt slip to the ground and Roy Tucker's spikes make a nervous sound as they scraped across the floor. He saw Elmer McCaffrey's lips tighten and a frown come over Harry's dark face. "You see, you fellas, this isn't just one kid, here, now. It isn't only Jocko Klein you guys are riding. I wonder can I make you understand? This boy Klein isn't yeller. He's a fighter, only he isn't fighting any of you. He's fighting two thousand years."

Did they understand? Did he understand? Or was Klein right when he said that an outsider could never understand?

"Now all this has gotta stop. As long as I'm manager, all you boys will make Jocko Klein feel he's one of us. He came up, same as you did, the hard way, and I want you to get behind him. Let's show him we're with him. He's not yeller, you take my word for that; you'll maybe find it out, you fellas, sooner than you think for. Just remember, he came up the hard road like you did; remember how it was when you broke in, Roy, and you, too, Karl, and you, Swanny, and you, Fat Stuff. That is, if you can remember that far back!"

The tension broke. A smile swept over the room, but there was no smile on the face of the manager's brother. Nuts, thought the second baseman, nuts to all that! Now he's giving them the stuff he tried to give me. Nuts!

"Now I believe this boy has the makings of a real, first-class ballplayer, and I don't intend to stand by and watch him ruined, either. That's what you're doing, you're ruining him. Oh, I know. I know you didn't any of you start out to do it. But that's how it works out. See here, this can be carried too far. Fun's fun. Sure, everyone must take kidding on a club; that's part of baseball. But what you boys are doing is . . ." He paused and looked round the room at the serious faces below . . . "murder. You heard me, murder. I know he's weak when it comes to a question of his race. O.K., you guys are using it to destroy his confidence. You're also destroying the team. You can't afford to do that. We've got a chance if everyone helps. Help me, boys, give me your support on this. Don't walk out on me over a personal difference. One thing I'm telling you—from now on this Jew-boy stuff is out. Do you all get it? Do I make myself clear on this?"

They swarmed onto the field, most of them thinking, Yes, that's correct. That's right. We gotta give the kid a chance. Under the earnest persuasion of the manager it sounded convincing, but once away from him and out of the locker room, it was clear that the team was still split. As Karl and Bob walked out together, Karl was saying, "Sure, that's all fine enough. Only after all, this isn't a reform school; it's a ballclub. If a guy can't help himself, what I say is we oughta get another catcher; that's how I see it."

"You betcha, and quick, too, Karl," Bob rejoined. "Boy, you got something there."

The division was apparent. On the side of the manager were the older men, Fat Stuff and McCaffrey and Swanson, and also young Roy Tucker.

Why, we didn't realize Klein was going to

pieces over all this foolishness. Aw, what the hell! Give the kid his chance.

On the other side were Karl and Rats Doyle and Bob Russell. Bob was thrashing it out at dinner with Roy Tucker that night, the center fielder trying hard to win him over.

"Why, sure, Roy, I guess I'd agree. Maybe we are ruining him. But we couldn't do it if he didn't let us. If a guy really hasn't got it . . . well . . ."

"But, Bob, we know he has. Give him a chance. We've seen him play, haven't we? He's got a pair of hands like shovels, he's got a great arm, and he can hit. That is, he could before we started in on him. With the team on him this way, nobody could play good ball. It doesn't take much to get a rookie down when he's breaking in. I recall back when Dave Leonard was managing the club, before Ginger Crane . . ."

"Spike and I were just coming up to the Vols from Dallas that year. I remember hearing them talk about Leonard."

"He was a great guy. A real ballplayer's ballplayer. Well, that first year . . . no, come to think it was the second year. The first year I was pitching and busted my elbow. Then I came back and tried to make the grade as an outfielder. I remember striking out coupla times in an important game against the Giants and getting low and feeling no good at all, and Dave Leonard caught me that night in my room packing to go home.

" 'Aha,' he says. 'Gonna quit, are you? So you're gonna quit the club,' he says. 'Can't take it, can you? You were gonna whang that pineapple out of the park this afternoon, an' you struck out. Then you go to pieces. Can't take it! Well, boy, don't forget one thing when you get back on that-there farm up in Connecticut. I come from a fishing country, and there's a saying down my way, "Only the game fish swim upstream".' "

"Yeah. That's it! That's the whole point, Roy. You had what it takes, you were dead game, you stuck it out. This guy quits cold. Now if he was really game, if only he really had it . . ."

"No, I wasn't. Any more than he is. I was all set to cut and run, only old Leonard came up that night and stopped me; made me so mad I cussed him out and stayed on to spite him. Let's give this kid a chance. Maybe if you had Karl Case and the bench jockeys in the other dugout and the fans and everyone yelling at you and calling you Jew-boy, maybe you'd crack, too. If only someone like Leonard or Fat Stuff could talk with him. If they could explain the boys aren't on him because he's Jewish but because they think he's yellow. Look! You'd be for the guy, wouldn't you, if he shows he has it?"

"Sure, if he does. But he hasn't yet. Spike's talked to him; so has Fat Stuff. Nope, it's no darn good, Roy, it's no good. Now the bird is upsetting the whole team; he's got us all split, and he's worried Spike until he can't sleep nights. His timing's off, too, way off. Notice he's started to back up for those balls to deep short. A guy with a Gatling gun for an arm couldn't do that; you're handing the runner first base when you do that. And this afternoon on that double-play ball in the sixth, a perfect doubleplay set-up with a slow man on first and no one to bust up the play, to kick me around on second. D'ja notice him on that one? All the time in the world, yet he straightens up for the throw and it was four feet high. He straightened up for the toss, something he never used to do. I was lucky to grab it at all. Why, Klein's even breaking up our combination. I wish he'd never come to this club, that's what I wish."

At the same time the manager was eating dinner with his rookie catcher in a small restaurant, trying to help him, to build him up, working on his confidence, probing for those sources of hidden strength which he knew must be there ready to spring up if they could only be properly tapped. They finished their meal, Spike talking and questioning him.

"My dad? I hardly knew him. My dad was in the butcher business in K.C. He died a long while ago; my mother brought me up."

"Say! That's funny. My pop died when I was young, and the Old Lady brought us up, too."

"That so? My ma kept a boarding-house for butchers and men who worked in the stock-yards."

"Why, for crying out loud! My ma kept a boarding-house in Charlotte for railway men; we never played ball until after she died."

"Then she never saw you up here?"

"Nope, never."

"Gee, that's tough. You know how 'tis, if you don't remember your pa and your ma brings you up. You're closer to her, sort of. Now my ma, she thinks I'm the greatest ballplayer on earth. Spike, you wouldn't hardly believe it. She has a scrapbook and I betcha she has fifty pictures of me." His eyes sparkled, his voice was deeper, his face flushed. The manager watched, listened, understood.

"Look, Jocko-boy, tell me something. You don't ever think of yer ma as a Jew, do you?"

The boy was startled. No one had ever asked him such a question. "Why, no, of course not."

"Fine. That's what you must do then, that's what you must do all the time. You gotta think of yourself as a catcher, not as a Jew. Get me? You gotta quit this thinking of yourself as a Jew first and a catcher on this-here team second. The last two thousand years, they don't matter. See, this is today, it's now. It's not even when you were nine years old; it's right now. You're a ballplayer, first and all the time. And as long as I'm manager I'll stick by you, 'cause I think you'll deliver and be a valuable man on the club. And as long as I do, you're the catcher of the Dodgers."

The catcher of the Dodgers! The catcher of the Dodgers, he thought . . .

"Now get this! When anyone rides you, anybody, the bench jockeys, the coaches, the Cubs, the Cards, the Braves, or Case and those boys there, remember one thing. You're not anything but the catcher of the Dodgers. Forget that dugout, forget those other teams, go out there and play ball like your ma thinks you can.

Like I know you can. Like the catcher of the Dodgers."

The manager rose. He was going back to his room where his brother would be waiting, knowing exactly how he had spent the evening, leering a little when he returned. But he was leaving behind a different person. Jocko Klein was still a freshman in the league, still the prey of the bench jockeys, the butt of every coach in every club on the circuit. Yet he was slowly beginning to think of himself as the catcher of the Dodgers again.

They were having batting practice the next morning before the game. Fat Stuff was tossing them up to the hitters. Behind him stood Charlie Draper, with the leather bag, feeding him balls. Each player went up for his raps, Tucker, Swanny, Bob, Roth, Allen.

At last came the turn of the rookie catcher. He stepped to the left side of the plate, and as he did so Case strode up to the other side. With the flat of his big hand he caught the boy full on the chest and shoved him away. Off balance, the catcher was sent reeling ten feet back, his bat slipping from his grasp.

"Get outa the way, you kike you; get outa the way and let a man hit that can."

The rookie tottered, stumbled, then found his feet. Old Fat Stuff in the box stood watching; the crowd around the batting cage came alive. Everyone realized something was going to break at last. It did. The boy reacted quickly. He grabbed the nearest bat and, turning, was at the plate in three strides.

"Look, Case." He waved the club at the astonished fielder. "That stuff's over. I'm the catcher of the Dodgers, get it? If you wanna slug it out, O.K."

His voice was loud and harsh. It carried to Fat Stuff, hands on hips by the mound, to Charlie Draper, open-mouthed behind him, to Bob, perched on second, even to Spike, watching anxiously in deep short.

"That's out . . . over . . . understand?"

They stood face to face, jaw to jaw, exactly as they had stood along the first base line the week before. For a moment neither moved; they remained, each with a bat in his hands, waiting. A show-down had come at last. Who would hit first? Or would they drop their bats and go for each other with fists? The whole field watched.

But this time something had changed. It was the burly fielder who was astonished and on the defensive, the rookie who was hard and unafraid. Case hesitated. He started to lay on with his bat, to go for the fresh young busher, when his eyes rested on Klein's hands. They were white and tense around the handle of that club; they looked as if he meant business. The big chap glanced down at the stocky figure across the plate, at those hands tightening around the handle. What he saw he didn't care for.

He shrugged his shoulders. "O.K.," he murmured casually. "O.K., pal." Then he moved away.

Klein swung his club nervously in his fists and resumed his batting stance. For a second or two no one moved; the entire field was a motion picture stopped in action. Then Fat Stuff turned and held up his glove to Charlie for a ball. He got it, wound up, and threw it in. The boy clouted it with fierceness. There was relief in that gesture, the relief of hitting something at last. The ball sailed away into the bleachers in center field. Fat Stuff turned again, asked for another ball, and this time wound up carefully, throwing a high inside pitch. The boy stepped deftly back and caught it squarely. It was high, very high, and very deep. In fact it was clearing the fence; it was over in Bedford Avenue.

20

A Sunday crowd in the Polo Grounds. The Sunday crowd is no fun. Weekday fans are smarter; they come regularly and are more tolerant, they know their baseball. But three-fourths of the Sunday crowd were there for one thing—to see the Dodgers beaten. Furthermore, a Sunday crowd meant a capacity crowd and that meant a mass of white shirts in deep center field; hard for the batters when they face an overarm pitcher. A sidearm thrower is not so bad, but an overarm ball coming out of that white background is poison. For this reason the Giants were using Tommy Quinn, their overarm pitching ace.

Razzle was pitching for Brooklyn. Raz was invariably tough against the Giants, who years before had let him out as a rookie hurler up for trial. He wanted to beat them more than any other club. So up to the third inning it was a pitcher's battle all the way, a wickedly close game. One of those games to be won or lost by the breaks.

In the third Klein came up to bat accompanied by the usual jeers from the Giants' bench. The pitcher rocked in the box.

"Sit him down, Tommy, sit him down."

"Don't let that Jew-boy get a toehold up there, Tom."

"Brush him back, Tommy. He can't take it, Tom old boy . . ."

"He's a quitter, Tommy, he can't take it."

It was the usual chorus. But something had happened to Jocko Klein, as the Giant bench began to realize that afternoon. The big pitcher leaned back and threw a fast ball, a duster that was close to Klein's chin and sent him sprawling back in the dirt. While Spike from the lines at third watched nervously, the chorus of approval rose from the jockeys in the Giants' bench.

"That's the stuff, Tom old boy. This guy's a pushover."

Tommy Quinn's duster was usually thrown with a purpose. He liked to set up the batter for the next pitch. The rookie knew this, knew it would be a curve, got ready for the hook and waited. It came, low, right where he expected, and he slammed it hard into the slot between short and third. The jeers from the home bench died abruptly away.

Razzle, who followed, struck out. Now came the top of the batting order. Spike gave the sign for a hit-and-run and Swanny responded with a dry, crisp drive into right field. Ballplayers all hope to get from first to third on a hit to right. In right field, however, was Jake Schott, the Giant captain, with the best throwing arm in the league.

Although Klein was off with the ball, the hit was clean and straight. Spike measured the distance, weighing that remorseless throwing arm against the speed of his rookie catcher, balancing in an instant the closeness of the score, the importance of getting that first run, the run which might even win the game. He called the boy on to third.

Straining, giving everything, with taut face and tensed muscles, Klein came in.

"Slide . . . Jocko . . . slide, boy," shouted Spike. "Slide . . . get down . . ."

The throw was coming straight and true like all Jake's throws, gaining on the runner. The man and the ball arrived simultaneously. Once again it was a matter of seconds, of fractions of a second. Klein's feet went out in a whirl of dust, and he made a desperate stab for the corner of the base with one foot as the man above reached down with the ball in his gloved fist.

The hand of the umpire started to rise. Then something happened. Was it accident, was it chance, was it on purpose that Klein came in with his spikes flashing in the sun? You saw their sudden glint, then the third baseman was hastily shaking his hand and the ball was bobbling on the grass behind the foul line.

Instantly Klein was up. He was up and away. The man on the base turned angrily, saw the ball back of the bag, darted after it. Again it was fractions of a second, but this time the throw was hurried and less accurate. Sliding head first for the outer corner, the rookie reached home for the first score of the game.

The Giants didn't like it at all. Who would? You call a man yellow, and he makes third against the best arm in the business, and slugs and kicks his way home for the only run of the game. A run that inning after inning kept getting bigger and bigger. No, the Giants didn't like it in the least. They showed it plainly enough in the sixth when, with two out, they loaded the bases and the fans stood roaring for them to score.

Spike trotted across the grass to Razzle. The big chap was cool and undisturbed. He shook off the boy at his side with a reassuring nod, stepped off the mound to catch the signs better, the only calm person in the feverish ballpark. Then he hitched at his pants, stepped back on the mound and stood there, his long arms hanging down motionless. He looked around the bases, at the infield playing deep for the force-out, at the outfield slightly around toward right for the batter. Then he threw. The man at the plate swung a trifle late and while the field started into motion, the ball sailed in the air.

It was a pop-up, a foul fly. Klein's mask was on the ground, his head upturned, as he twisted and then started toward the Giant bench. Close, closer, closer. So close it was dangerous. None of the Giants called or warned him.

"Look out, Jocko, look out, Jocko!" Spike's voice was drowned in the uproar as the catcher went on. Don't tell me that guy isn't a ballplayer! Boy, is he a ballplayer!

His upturned face followed the ball, his mitt was close to his chest as it descended. Now he was on the edge of the step. He tottered, held out his mitt, caught the ball, and fell heavily into the mass of scattering players below.

There was a moment's delay. Then he limped slowly out of the dugout with the ball in his fist.

So into the seventh, the eighth, the ninth. The run which had looked big earlier in the game now looked as big as a thousand. Pinch hitters came in for the Giant pitchers, relief men took the mound, runners were substituted for slow men on the bases. Still the score remained one to nothing.

Then the end, the last of the ninth, with the crowd screaming for a score, a run, only one run to tie it up and send the game into extra innings. The Giants got a man as far as second with one out. The Giant captain then came to bat and hit a long, lazy single to center field.

The runner on second was the Giant third baseman who had lost the ball and then made the wide throw to the plate to let Klein score. He was out for blood. Waved on by the coach at third, he set sail for home, head down, his arms swinging, determined to score if he killed someone. But he was competing against another throwing arm as good as anyone's in the league. Roy Tucker, charging in took the ball on the first hop and threw smoothly to the plate. It needed a better than average throw to beat that runner, and the center fielder delivered just that—a throw waist high, right on a line into Klein's mitt.

The Giant runner, ten feet away, heard the plop of the ball in the glove even before he could start his slide. He knew he was out, knew his team was beaten, knew a slide was futile. So angrily he hurled himself at the catcher. Klein was braced to meet the shock and protect the plate; but even so the force and fury of that charging drive was too powerful. The Giant came in, knee up. Klein tagged him and then shot away. There was a bump, a bump you could hear all over the field, a bump that would have lifted anyone but a rugged catcher clean out of the ballpark. As it was, Klein went sprawling head over heels in the dirt beside the plate.

With agony Spike watched from the cut-off position halfway to the box. Hold it, Jocko; hold that ball, kid. Hold it and you're the people's choice, you can run for president in Brooklyn.

He held it. He had it in one clenched fist. He waved it in the air and then tossed it away. He was going into the Giant player with everything he had.

"Well . . . fer cryin' . . . out . . . loud!" Inside the clubhouse old Chiselbeak, his arms full of dirty towels, paused in mid-passage. In the alcove, where Doc Masters sat on his rubbing table, was a small bench with a portable radio on it. From the radio came the fantastic story of Jocko Klein. No wonder Chiselbeak stood motionless, no wonder the Doc listened with open mouth. Klein, the Jewish catcher of the Dodgers, was in a fight.

". . . Boy-oh-boy . . . they're slugging it out now, all right . . . there's a punch . . . and another . . . Taylor lets him have it with both barrels on the jaw . . . Casey, the plate umpire, jumped Klein . . . the catcher shook him off like a rat . . . now other players are rushing up . . . but the two men are still slugging . . . they're really slugging now . . . they're in close . . . wow! . . . wow! . . . was that a punch! Oh, what a sock . . . Klein gave it to him hard . . . and again . . . there goes Taylor . . . he's tumbling . . . he's down . . . he's out . . . and sixteen men have jumped Jocko Klein and yanked him away . . .

"Just hear that roar over the ballpark . . . hear that crowd howl . . . hear them go . . . wait a minute . . . I think . . . yes . . . there it comes . . . there it comes . . . the old heave-ho . . . the old heave-ho for Klein . . . there goes Klein . . . off the field for him . . . boy, will he get a fine slapped on him for this afternoon's work!"

No wonder Chiselbeak stood there motionless with the dirty towels in his arms; no wonder the Doc sat with his mouth open, as they both listened. No wonder both were speechless.

Then the outer door opened and a figure appeared. He was dirty, he was wet, his monkey suit was torn, the strap of one shin guard had broken and flapped ridiculously at his heel, his face was strangely red. As he entered he wiped his forehead with the back of his hand, leaving it smeared with blood. His eyes were swollen, his cheeks and his jaw were raw and bruised.

The towels were slipping from old Chiselbeak's arms. "Well, fer cryin' . . . out . . . loud, Jocko! Fer cryin' out . . . loud!"

21

The team stepped from the express at North Philadelphia the next morning into an oven. The heat reached out and slapped them in their faces as they left the air-conditioned train. Taxis were fireless cookers. The dressing room at Shibe Park was a steam bath. Someone with a newspaper remarked that it was the hottest July twenty-seventh in Philadelphia for eighteen years.

The heat destroyed you, beat you down. Even under the roof of the dugout you sat gratefully on a towel, wondering how the bullpen pitchers could stand it out there in the sun in deep right field. As usual there was a sparse crowd scattered through the big double-decked stadium; you expected sparse crowds playing the Phils. But the torment of the weather was bad, and for the Dodgers it was accentuated by three rabid fans who sat just above the dugout.

This trio, huge fellows in their shirtsleeves, spent the afternoon amusing themselves by pounding on the roof of the Dodger dugout with empty pop bottles and needling the Brooklyn players as they went up to and returned from the plate.

The strain had begun to tell. After that hard-fought victory over the Giants of the previous afternoon there was a let-down, and the Phillies were making the most of it. They scored once in the third, knocked McCaffrey out of the box in the fourth by scoring two more runs, and hit Rog Stinson for a couple more in the sixth.

Losing to a team in first or second place is one thing; but you hardly figure to drop games to the Phils so easily. To make things worse, toward the closing innings that pound-pound-pound above their heads became as agonizing to the tired nerves of the Dodgers as the tom-tom of savages in the African jungle. In the field reliable players like Harry Street let grounders go through or mis-timed pop flies. While at the plate the whole batting order was tied up in knots.

Especially annoying was the hammering of the fans at Jocko Klein. A week before, perhaps even a few days before, the shouting of the fans would have been taken philosophically as part of the game. But a few days had passed, and the feeling of the team had changed. They felt differently; they had to feel differently since he had licked the Giants almost single-handed the day before and had become a fighting, scrapping ballplayer. As the Dodgers returned to the bench after the end of the seventh, the three fans became more raucous than before. Spike moved over to Paul Roth, telling him to be ready to take his raps for the pitcher if a rally should start. In front of the dugout Klein, on one knee, was unbuckling his shin-guards. The fans in the box above saw him and burst into a frenzy of abuse.

"Aw . . . yer Jew-boy, you're yeller, ya big bum."

"Yer yeller kike, look out there or he'll pare yer beak offa ya."

It was too much. Half the team were instantly on the step of the dugout, holding on to the roof, looking up toward the leather-lunged lunatics in the box above. The catcher, his back turned, his neck crimson, stood up to unfasten the straps of his chest protector.

"Yer yeller, Klein, ya know ya are."

Bob Russell, standing beside Swanny, felt himself getting warmer than the weather. It was too much.

"Hey there, you guys," he shouted. "Lay off! Cut that out!"

It was exactly what the fans wanted, the first sign all afternoon that their needling of the team had any effect. In unison the three thumped the dugout roof with their empty pop bottles, and one large shirt-sleeved figure rose from his chair.

"Come up and make us, ya bum, ya."

"Lissen, mug," yelled another, "if you don't like it ya know whatcha can do, don't ya?"

"Hey there, Klein," shrieked a third. "You're yeller, you know you are; you can't take it, you Jew-boy."

That settled it. They were a team and one of the team was under fire. It was time to act.

"Come on, boys," said the second baseman of the Dodgers. Grasping the edge of the dugout he hauled himself up with one motion and scrambled over the roof toward the box and those shrieking fans.

Now Bob Russell was a favorite with everyone on the club. A manager can't have favorites or be a favorite either. But the whole team loved their peppery little second baseman, and they didn't intend to watch him go into battle alone. Right on his heels were big Swanson and Harry Street. And Raz Nugent. And Roy Tucker, death in his eyes, armed with a formidable looking fungo stick.

Fists flew. So did bats, chairs, rolled newspapers, anything which could be used as a weapon. The three fans fell before the onslaught of the furious Dodgers. Not, however, without a struggle. It was one of the best free-for-all fights in baseball history, involving players, fans, ushers, attendants, policemen, and various customers from the vicinity who couldn't bear to see a fight without mixing in. In three minutes the boxes above the Brooklyn dugout resembled a tank battlefield. All the while the cause of the encounter was sitting quietly on the bench underneath, waiting for the game to continue and his turn at bat to come round.

Finally the smoke of battle cleared away. The loud-mouthed fans were rushed off by policemen and green-uniformed attendants, and the players led by Bob Russell, scarred but happy, climbed down from the boxes, over the dugout roof and back inside, bearing an assortment of abrasions, contusions, and lacerations as evidence of the conflict. Most of the crowd was unaware of the exact cause of the battle; but ball crowds love a fight, a fight in plain view on the diamond against the visitors or the umpires if possible; yet any kind of a fight is better than none. When Swanny stepped to the plate he was greeted with applause.

He responded by smacking the first pitch to the left for a single.

Red Allen immediately singled, too.

Roy Tucker came up. He looked dangerous and was passed, filling the bases.

Now the sparse, apathetic crowd was up yelling, and the Phillies' catcher and pitcher met together in the middle of the path down to the mound. Karl Case waited for a full count and then tripled to the barriers, four hundred feet from the plate, clearing the bases.

A new hurler came rapidly across from the bullpen to stifle the Dodger rally. Harry Street promptly greeted him with a scorching double down the left field line. In the coaching box back of third, Spike felt the whole team begin to move at last, to move as a team.

Gosh, something has happened. Something has given way. Something has broken the tension. Now we're really moving. We're off at last!

Bob came up to the plate and worked a base on balls. Then Jocko Klein ambled forward. The whole Dodger dugout was on the step, not one or two or a few, but all of them—the subs, the players, the relief pitchers, even old Chiselbeak who had come out from the lockers with a towel over his shoulders, all yelling through their hands. All behind the boy in the batter's box.

"Give us a hit, Jocko . . ."

"You can do it, you can do it, Jocko old kid . . ."

"Put one up in Aunt Minnie's room . . ."

"All right, Klein old boy, here comes the big one . . . the big one coming, Jocko . . ."

The Philadelphia pitcher saw them shouting, looked around nervously at the men on first and second, took the signs. He felt the team backing the man at the plate, felt he was not only trying to outguess one hitter but facing the whole club, determined and united. The boy felt it, too, felt the rise of team spirit, heard above the noise of the stands the voices of men he knew. There was a ring to them, a sound he had never heard before. This was it. This was it at last. They fought for me up there in the boxes; they're with me. I'm the catcher of the Dodgers now!

He was warm all over and not from the burning sun either. He gripped his bat, gripped it hard. Let's see your pay pitch, big boy. I'm ready for it.

The man in the box slowed up on him. He swung hard for a strike. The shouts from behind were louder than ever. Then the pitcher tried foolishly to sneak one over. It was an outside corner fast ball, the one he wanted. He gave everything he had.

From the shade in the coaching box back of third base Spike stood on tiptoes watching the ball in the haze of the afternoon. Oh, boy, he pickled that one . . . I think . . . I hope . . . yessir . . . the kid sure pickled that one!

The Phillie right fielder was burning up the ground, tearing desperately back for the catch, running hard for the fence, getting ready to turn and jump, slowing down, standing there panting, his arms on his hips, his head in the air. The ball descended slowly over the right field wall.

22

He came out of the tiny dressing room adjoining the larger one, and stood in the doorway looking over the roomful of naked, half-naked, and half-dressed players. Tommy Heeney of the *Eagle* walked past and spoke.

"Well, Spike, those three games over in Philadelphia sort of set you up, hey?"

"Uhuh." When you don't say anything, as Grouchy often remarked, you don't ever have to eat your own words.

"You've won four games straight."

"That's correct."

"Your biggest winning streak of the season, isn't it? If you grab this off today you'll be in fifth place."

"That's correct."

"Think you can win the pennant, Spike?"

It was meant, as he knew, for a joke or possibly the foundation of a wisecrack in Heeney's column the next morning. But Spike Russell, trained in a hard school, in Grouchy's school, merely answered, "We gotta chance."

Not much there. The sportswriter passed along, leaving the manager leaning against the door, surveying his team as they got ready for the Cards in that critical series which might make or break them for the year. Ordinarily he would have held a meeting. Ordinarily he would have gone over their hitting, cautioned his men about their playing, about the importance of every game now. Not today. This team was keen. This team was ready to go.

He tried to look at them objectively, men he knew, had liked, admired, loved, disliked, or hated at various times; men he had, he hoped, finally succeeded in molding into what was called a team. And what was a team? It was everything in sport and in life, yet nothing you could touch or see or feel or even explain to someone else. A team was like an individual, a character, fashioned by work and suffering and disappointment and sympathy and understanding, perhaps not least of all by defeat.

A team was made up of equal parts of Bob's pep and fire and vinegar mixed with Roy's quiet determination when things went wrong. It was those big flat muscles on Rats Doyle's stomach as he pulled on his shirt. It was the warm friendly way in which Red Allen was putting surgeon's plaster on a blister along Harry's thumb. It was Karl Case's drive and push in the clutch when he forgot his batting average and was trying hard to win for the club. It was Raz Nugent's imagination which kept them laughing off the field. It was Fat Stuff's reliability. It was the nervous power of Swanny straining for an impossible low liner that was sinking fast, a liner most men would have played safe as a hit. It was the harnessed energy of Elmer McCaffrey when he was bearing down in a difficult situation. It was the courage of Jocko Klein, sliding into the plate on his stomach, hands out to be chewed by the spikes of the catcher defending home plate above. It was all these men and all these qualities that made a team.

He knew them, knew them all, knew them even better than their parents, better than their wives and children would ever know them. He saw them when only the man showed through, when all defenses were down, when nothing counted except what they had underneath. He knew them best, yet there were things about them that even Spike Russell did not know and could never know.

He knew that in the crisis of a game, in the late afternoon when the shadows covered him, Harry Street was the most dependable th' 'd baseman in the league. He did not know that a Calvinist named Herald van Stirum fought in the religious wars at Leyden in the low countries or that his son would join a band of men who called themselves Pilgrims, and end up across an ocean in the New World. He knew Elmer McCaffrey would go out on the mound with a lame arm or a bad side and pitch his heart out until he had to be hauled away from the mound, that he would stand there stubbornly in the last innings with the bases full and a slugger at bat, suffering so he could hardly breathe yet insisting he was all right. But he didn't know that the McCaffreys were fierce Catholics, one of whom died under Charles First fighting Cromwell at Marston Moor. Nor that his descendant still in kilts, kilts of khaki, dirty and brown, but kilts nevertheless, was overrun by the hordes of the

Mahdi and fell near Gordon on the steps of the Palace at Khartoum.

Spike realized that of all the team Swanny was the most daring, but he did not realize that this was in his blood, that it came from a man with a flowing yellow mane who went into battle singing hymns with Gustavus II at Lutzen.

Nor did Spike know that in '62 a boy named Tucker marched off from a New England farm to die with the Second Connecticut Volunteers at Cedar Creek in the Shenandoah Valley, nor that the regiment against them was the Third North Carolina State Troops commanded by a man named Russell. Although he knew a Russell was an officer in the Confederate army, he did not know that a peppery, leather-lunged little fellow full of fire and spirit fought beside Andrew Jackson on the shell-swept rampart of the Rodriguez Canal at New Orleans. He didn't know that a red-bearded man named Allen had piled his family and goods into a wagon after the Civil War and, with his rifle on his knees, whipped up his horses and started west. Over the Mississippi, through the frontier regions of the Middle Border, out into the desolate prairie where you had to be ready for anything, across the Rockies and into the sunbaked lands along the Pacific. Spike did not know this. He would have been surprised to learn that Red Allen came from men who were quick on the draw, that some of his courage and alertness came from men who had been used to facing danger.

Most of all, Spike would have been astonished to hear the story of Israel Klein. Long, long ago Israel Klein had been a trader in the ghettos of Marrakesh in Morocco, a man who bargained with the ship captains from the ports along the Atlantic. He had become known in the city as an established merchant, but his home, his business, and his goods were lost when Berbers sacked the town and captured it. Escaping with his family, he finally reached Paris where again he established himself as a trader, again built up a business. In the reign of Philippe the Fair he was killed when members of his race were either murdered or banished from France. But his son escaped, and later an Israel Klein was doing business in Bavaria, where he flourished and handed on a profitable industry to his children. There they lived, worked, raised families, and died, until 1550. Then they, also, were exiled. So the Israel Kleins moved along as they had been moving for centuries, from Bavaria north to the Hanseatic States on the sea; from place to place, from country to country, through a "river of blood and time," building up trade, working, prospering, then losing their freedom again, suffering, dying. Until one day in the ghetto of Vienna, a descendant of old Israel Klein of Marrakesh heard of a new land, a land where persecutions did not exist, or banishments or pogroms, where children were not sold into slavery or families destroyed.

These were some of the things Spike did not know about his team, the team that was lost and found itself. For now they were a team, all of them. Thin and not so thin, tall and short, strong and not so strong, solemn and excitable, Calvinist and Covenanter, Catholic and Lutheran, Puritan and Jew, these were the elements that, fighting, clashing and jarring at first, then slowly mixing, blending, refining, made up a team. Made up America.

"Hey, youse . . ."

Back in the Dodger clubhouse on Ebbets Field, the team was moving out to the diamond. Clack-clack, clackety-clack, clack-clack, clackety-clack; there was a note of confidence in the way their spikes resounded on the concrete walk.

"Hey, youse, there's a ballgame on!"

Old Chiselbeak gave him an affectionate shove toward the door.

Gosh, yes. Spike had forgotten about Chiselbeak. Old Chisel, the man no one ever saw, who took your dirty clothes and handed out clean towels and cokes, and packed the trunks and kept the keys to the safe and did the thousand things no one ever saw. Chisel was part of the team, too; and, though Spike didn't realize it as he followed his team along the concrete runway, part of America also. He was the millions and millions who never have their names in the line-up, who never play before the crowd, who never hit home runs and get the fans' applause; who work all over the United States, underpaid, unknown, unrewarded. The Chiselbeaks are part of the team, too.

23

Stanley King of the *Telegram* sauntered across behind the plate where half the Cardinals were gathered around the batting cage, over to their dugout on the other side of the diamond. There was a small space beside Grouchy, and Stanley squeezed into it. The Cardinal manager gave him a grunt which could have meant anything from a none too cordial greeting to a suggestion that he move along down the bench to the empty spaces at the other end. Stanley, like all good reporters, was obtuse to hints.

"Just spoke to Spike Russell. Thinks he might win the pennant."

"He's gotta chance," said the old fellow, peering out with practiced eyes on his charges scattered over the sunswept field.

This was so exactly what Spike had said that Stanley had to smile. "Why? Because they won three straight from the Phils?"

"They all count in the win column."

"So they tell me. But it isn't hard to lick a last-place club. Besides, the Russells aren't clicking. When the Russells don't click, those Dodgers aren't anything better than a seventh place team. They were muffing doubleplays last week, you know, snatching at the ball before they had it."

"That's bad timing. They'll snap out of it. They're good kids."

"They better—and soon," rejoined Stanley. "They certainly aren't clicking now."

"I'll believe it when I see it," said Grouchy, skeptical as always. He rose and strolled away. Whenever possible he deprived himself of the pleasure of long conversations, especially with sportswriters.

The Dodgers got away to a good start, scoring two runs in the first inning on long drives to the fence by Case and Swanny; but Rats Doyle was being hit frequently all through the early part of the game. In the third, with men on first and second and one down, the Card batter smacked a scorching grounder slightly to Bob's right. It was beautiful to see him swoop down on the ball, to watch his right foot directly in its path, his left so placed that the instant he had it he could turn and throw underhand to his brother on second. One moment it was bouncing toward him, then it was gone, it was Spike's, it was Red's. And the Dodgers were tossing their gloves behind them and racing back again to the shelter of the bench.

Sometimes two runs look big; but that afternoon they were an infinitesimal edge, so small you hardly could see them. For while the Card pitcher handcuffed the hitters after that opening inning and got better as he went along, Rats Doyle was in trouble from the start. There were men on bases every inning, and only good support kept them from scoring. You could see the relief on the face of the big pitcher as the Keystone Kids got him out of one hole after another. In the fourth, however, two men singled with the top of the Cardinal batting order at the plate and only one out. So Spike signaled for Elmer McCaffrey. Elmer was a good relief pitcher with runners on base; he threw underhand and had a first-class sinker that kept the ball low. Elmer tossed in his warm-up pitches. He hoisted his belt, looked round the diamond, and went to work.

Then the fans were on their feet yelling, the diamond became a meaningless jig-saw puzzle, and men were running in every direction, because the ball was going through. It was past, it would go through, when suddenly Spike made a running dive, his glove on the end of that long arm stabbing for the ball and holding it. For just a tiny moment he was off balance, legs apart as he tried to pivot and make the throw. The toss came to his brother waiting on the bag; next the throw burning into first. Once more they were running toward the bench instead of standing on the field with a run across and first and third occupied by enemy players.

In the sixth the Card lead-off man singled. Elmer walked the following batter; two on and nobody down. Nervously Spike glanced toward the bullpen, watching the activity there with relief. The third man flied out to Roy in center, but the next man rapped a long single to Swanny. The blond fielder came charging in, played the ball cleanly on the first hop, and made a perfect throw to Bob on second base.

And the Cardinal runner from first was halfway down the path toward third.

Bob snapped a quick one to his brother who ran over and tagged the hesitating runner. Then he threw back again to Bob. The little second baseman turned, saw the runner coming into the base from first and nailed him on the slide. One run was across, but again the side was retired. Grouchy, sitting on the bench and watching St. Louis players cut down and rallies snuffed out, began to lose patience. He shook his head. "When they're hitting on all four, those Russell boys can't be beat," he remarked to a player beside him.

Meanwhile Elmer held the Cardinals hitless in the seventh, was saved in the eighth by two marvelous catches by Roy Tucker, one in deep center against the bleacher wall. Those blows had the ring of authority, and with each one Spike's gaze turned toward the bullpen, watching Fat Stuff starting his throws close up to old Kenny, the bullpen catcher, then moving back, further back. The manager could almost hear Kenny's voice, almost hear him thumping his mitt, urging the pitcher on in his warm-up. "C'mon now, c'mon, Fat Stuff . . . get hot, boy . . ." Thump-thump. Thump-thump. "C'mon, get hot, boy . . . get hot . . ."

Two to one in the ninth. The first batter slashed a wicked bounder at Red behind first. He fielded the ball perfectly and gave Elmer a reassuring wave with his glove, a kind of pat in the air to let him know he had the putout and to save him from running over to cover the bag.

"O.K., gang, le's go . . . le's go, gang, le's get this one." Bob tossed the ball to Spike and Spike shot it over to Red and Red burned it across to Harry Street, who rubbed it carefully and walked to the mound where he handed it to Elmer. One down.

Two outs and we've won five straight. C'mon, gang, le's go . . .

But the next man singled ominously. Only Karl Case's good fielding kept him on first.

Now what? Shall I yank Elmer or shan't I? We want this game, we need this game the worst way. To beat the league leaders right now would give this crowd just the confidence they need. This is where being manager is no fun.

Spike walked over to the mound. "How about it, Elmer? How you feel, boy?"

"Lemme get this one, Spike, Jes lemme throw to this one." So he threw, and the batter nearly decapitated him with a liner past his right ear. Men on first and second. Fat Stuff came shuffling over from the bullpen at last. He took the mound. Now everyone in the park was standing up.

"O.K., Fat Stuff . . ."

"O.K., O.K., Fat Stuff . . ."

"Alla time, Fat Stuff, alla time . . ."

"This is the easy one, Fat Stuff. Let him hit it, old-timer; we'll nail him for you."

Out there at short and second is where you have to talk things up in the tight moments of a game. But the chatter came also from Karl and Harry, from Roy and Jocko Klein. Everyone was on edge, the fans, the teams, even old Grouchy on the bench.

The ball was to Spike's right, the hardest ball the shortstop has to handle, the test of a great infielder. It all had to be done fast, too, the stop, the recovery, the throw. He got down to it and stayed down the way older men never could; he went down and nailed the ball. Picking it from the ground and throwing it was one continuous motion, a quick underhand snap which Bob from years of experience timed perfectly. He understood Spike, he expected Spike to give it to him where he wanted it, and Spike did, high enough and not too high. Bob expected it there because Spike was on the throwing end.

Bob gathered it in, and in his turn sent it off. Stretching out with all the reach of his large frame, Red Allen received the ball. The arm of the umpire beside second and then the arm of the man back of first rose in the air. The first baseman straightened up. With all his strength, with a kind of release and joy and something of a gesture of including all the team on the last play of the game, he twisted and shot the ball to Jocko Klein standing bareheaded at the plate.

Jocko let it slap into his mitt. Then he tossed it twenty feet high in the air before him. The ball fell to the ground between home and the pitcher's mound, unheeded as everyone dashed for the clubhouse.

Players poured off the field and fans poured on. Grouchy, meanwhile, picked his way through the mass outside his dugout and at the entrance to the stands joined his coach from third.

"Them Keystone Kids," he growled, "them Keystone Kids! Who told me them boys weren't clicking? What I say is, you can't never trust what you hear from sportswriters. Who said they'd lost it?" A long speech for Grouchy Devine.

When newspapermen desert a first-place ball-club to mob the dressing room of a fifth-place club, something is doing. Something had suddenly made the Dodgers news. It wasn't merely the victory; it was the way they won it and something more; something in their manner at bat and in the field, a confidence in the way they played that they hadn't had before. The sportswriters recognized the difference as they watched the game that afternoon, and that was why they all left Grouchy and his first-place Cards to crowd the lockers of the victorious team: the team that had slumped and degenerated into a sullen collection of ballplayers, that had pulled itself together and become a fighting unit again.

Though they didn't realize it, that's what the Dodgers were celebrating in the lockers—the re-birth of their team. The sportswriters knew it well enough, and wandered around, watching, listening, asking questions. Tommy Heeney and Stanley King and Ed Morgan and the rest were everywhere, talking now to this player now to another. So were those cagey, eagle-eyed men, the photographers. Wherever cameramen are, there is news. They came piling in after the team, adjusting their machines, setting bulbs in place, unscrewing them and putting them in their pockets, shoving and pushing through the crowd of hot, weary, happy ballplayers.

Over the room and above the noise of the showers and the opening and shutting of steel lockers came the voices of the victorious team.

"Nice chucking there, Fat Stuff . . ."

"Nice chucking yerself, Elmer . . ."

"Hey, what's that man Tucker eat for breakfast?"

"I'll say! You don't realize how darn good Roy is until you ask yourself how many balls get over his head in a season. He makes it all seem easy."

"Nice catching, Jocko . . ."

"You sure handled those pitchers, Jocko . . ."

"Nice work, Jock . . ."

"Nice work yourself, Swanny. Boy, are you fast getting in for those liners!"

"Yessir, great work, Swanny . . ."

"Great work yourself, Bob. You and Spike pulled this one out for us . . ."

Surrounded by a semi-circle of sportswriters, Spike heard his name and looked up. He was finishing a sentence. "Why, sure they been playing better baseball lately; that's not the reason; we're all pulling together, that's why we started to roll."

On the bench opposite was his brother, the best pivot man in the league, the best guy who ever lived.

"Right, Bobby?" He leaned over.

"That's correct, Spike." He leaned over, too, and held out his hand. The Keystone Kids shook on it.

There was a quick outburst from every photographer in the room and a sudden rush of cameramen toward them.

"Hold it!"

"Hold it there, Spike . . ."

"Just like that, Bob . . . just like that."

"Hold it, like that, Spike, jes' hold it a second, please . . ."

Flash! Flash! Flash! The bulbs exploded in a circle, sending little puffs of smoke into the room, while the cameramen snapped the Russell brothers, the keystone combination of the Dodgers.

John R. Tunis (1889–1975) was considered one of the finest writers for boys during the 1940s and 1950s. He played collegiate sports at Harvard, served in World War I, and after the war worked as a sportswriter and commentator, publishing articles in popular magazines such as *The New Yorker* and *The Saturday Evening Post*. It wasn't until 1938, when he was forty-nine, that he wrote the first of his more than twenty books for young people. That novel, *Iron Duke*, won the *New York Tribune*'s Spring Book Festival award, and many of his later novels were also award winners. Mr. Tunis's knowledge of sports, his attention to detail, and his concern over social issues give his novels a timeless relevance and appeal that have made them enduringly popular with readers of all ages.